Skyhawk crashes
San Diego
Santiango sings
Desert showdown
The Kiss
Frontier of Beasts
Tijuana
Río Grande
Gabriel's Race
Creel
Squirrel Soup
The Church
Sol and Rosalita fight
"Snow from the Moon"
N
S

Pancho's Song

a Hal Bradbury Adventure

By Tom Fremantle

Best wishes,

Tom

and

Pancho

To my childhood friends

Jim Fry

and

Geoff Goodman

Best mates then, best mates now

and

To my friends in Ciudad Juárez

A city with the worst of reputations and the best of people

EL PASO
COMMUNITY
FOUNDATION

Over three years ago the author of *Pancho's Song*, Tom Fremantle, walked 1,000 miles between Ciudad Juárez and San Diego, zigzagging between the Mexican and the American side of the border.

Tom was accompanied on his journey by a street dog from Juárez called Pancho. Everyone loved Pancho. He was the star of the show, completely outshining Tom. Indeed, he was *Shrek* and Tom was *Donkey*. Pancho is now one of the key characters in the book.

Although it is a complete work of fiction, *Pancho's Song* does touch on some USA-Mexico border issues such as gangs, the plight of migrant workers and the fence between the two countries. But, above all, it is an action-packed adventure story with plenty of humor.

The book also rejoices in the border and the resilience, courage and generosity of its people. Just the sort of people Tom and Pancho met on their travels. It is a book aimed at 11 year-olds plus but, with the gripping plot and fascinating characters, can equally be enjoyed by adults.

The proceeds of the book will go entirely to border charities including *Fundación Comunitaria de la Frontera Norte*, an NGO improving the lives of young people in Juárez; *Cruz Verde*, a superb emergency ambulance service and *Visión en Acción*, a ground-breaking refuge for the homeless. All three charities are small, inspiring places run exclusively by Mexicans. For more information on them, check out: **www.booksandblisters.com/charities/**

The book's publisher is *Border Giving Press* – a charitable initiative of the *El Paso Community Foundation* (EPCF). It is in many ways a unique project, with all the proceeds going to great border causes that the EPCF and the author wanted to support.

We hope you enjoy the book. Why not let us know what you think on Pancho's Facebook page: *'Pancho, the Canine Border Ambassador'* or on Amazon (in Mexico, America or the UK).

Many thanks! *¡Muchas gracias!*

About the author

Tom Fremantle is an author and adventurer. His previous books are *Johnny Ginger's Last Ride* (2000), about a 12,500 mile bicycle ride from England to Australia, *The Moonshine Mule* (2003), *The Road to Timbuktu* (2005) and *Nurse! Nurse!* (2011, under the pseudonym, *Jimmy Frazier*). *Pancho's Song* is his first novel.

Tom is a fellow of the *Royal Geographical Society* in London and has been described by the author, John Mortimer, as *'a writer who commands fascinated attention'* - and by his daughter, Eliza, as: *'quite good'*. He likes bicycles, mules and, of course, street dogs.

Chapters

Part One

The Sun and the Butterfly

Part Two

Mexico Bound
Lost in the Rain
Snow from the Moon
Miracles in Hell
Human Junkyard
Wrong Place / Wrong Time / Wrong Girl
The Cave
Señor Slimy
Marco the Narco

Part Three

The Sun Queen
Squirrel Soup
Running Wild
Flying Wild
Crash
Jerusalem
Pancho's Song
Showdown

Part Four

The Black Unicorn
Frontier of Beasts
Home

Epilogue

PART ONE

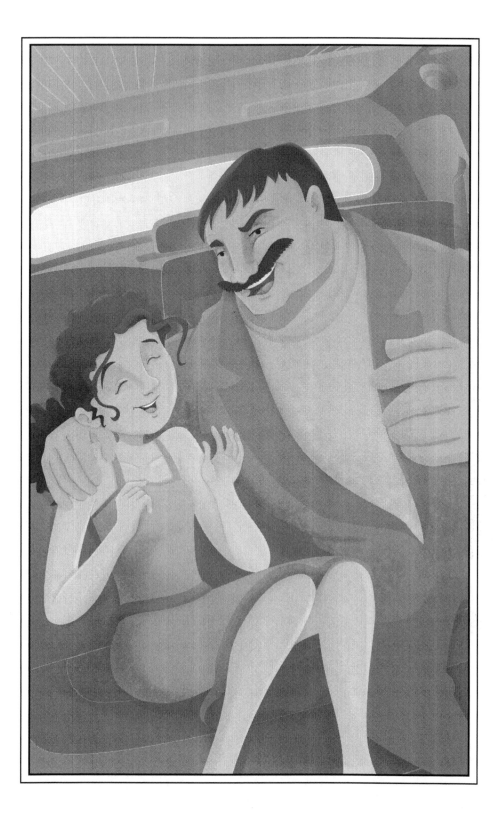

The Sun and the Butterfly

Cocooned in his bulletproof limo, Tomas Ceto, rubbed his moustache. It really was quite a moustache. Indeed, it was so big that his mouth was completely hidden under a fuzz of black, bushy bristles.

Mexico's Most Wanted Man liked the fact nobody could see his mouth: it meant nobody ever knew what he was thinking. Whether he was happy or sad, playing poker or about to shoot someone, the famous gangster's face rarely changed – his lips invisible, his eyes cold, his mind cunning.

Not much taller than a hobbit and with podgy cheeks it was easy to see why Tomas Ceto was known as *El Sapo* – The Toad. When he first read about this nickname, it made the violent killer's blood boil so much he stabbed his cigar into his laptop.

"Pah," he fumed, as the screen sizzled. "Since when did a toad ever boast a moustache like mine!"

But over time the nickname grew on him and now he rather liked it, knowing just a mention of *El Sapo* would strike terror into the hearts of his enemies –and he was a man with many, many enemies.

Anyway, thought Tomas Ceto as his limo weaved through the steamy, jam-packed streets of Mexico City, no one would call him The Toad to his face would they? Well, if they did, they wouldn't last long.

He stroked his moustache again, smug as a tomcat licking its whiskers, unawares that in less than five minutes, his whole world would be blown apart.

*

"You always play with your moustache, Papi," said Mariposa, smiling up at her father. "Especially when you're happy!"

Mariposa sat with her dad in the back of the limo while Sol, her elder sister, lay slumped in the passenger seat.

"You know me better than anyone, Mariposa," said Tomas Ceto, letting slip a grin. They were driving past an ancient cathedral, its bells chiming above them. "You are my guardian angel. My Little Butterfly."

He ruffled Mariposa's hair, which was long and dark and decorated with orange marigolds.

"And it's your birthday, Sweet Pea, my happiest day of the year. That's true isn't it, Señor Rodríguez?" Tomas Ceto asked the limo driver. "Mariposa's birthday is my favorite day!"

Señor Rodríguez was a crag-faced man, dressed all in black, who had been chauffeuring the Ceto family for over 20 years. He looked like a friendly vampire.

"Sure it's true, boss," replied the driver, turning and winking at Mariposa. As he smiled, his teeth glinted with gold. "And that was her best birthday party ever."

In the passenger seat Sol rolled her eyes in disgust. Never had two sisters been so at odds as Mariposa and Sol. In Spanish –the language of Mexico– Mariposa meant butterfly, and the birthday girl displayed much of that creature's impish grace.

Sol's name was much less suitable. It meant sun, but Mariposa's sister was certainly no sunbeam, preferring to spread an icy chill wherever she went. It was a joke among the Ceto family's many staff that Sol should never have been christened Sun – but Frosty Face or Thunder Girl.

16

It was clear she took after her father.

Mariposa was more like her mom, Carmen, a gentle beauty who had once loved to dance all night. Now, after being married to Tomas Ceto for many years, Carmen's nerves were in tatters. She stayed hidden away in the Ceto country ranch, too scared to show her face in the chaos of Mexico City where her husband had insisted on throwing Mariposa's party.

Sol, still fuming in the front seat, ripped off her iPod headphones and cursed the day Mariposa, her 'Sweet Pea' sister, had ever been born.

"So this is Papi's best day of the year," she thought bitterly, fondling a sun-shaped ring on her finger. "What about my birthday?"

Sol craved her father's love but Tomas Ceto only had eyes for his Little Butterfly. In truth, Mariposa had no idea that her Papi was a gangster. To her, he was someone who gave her endless presents, cuddles and ice creams and she adored him for it, as any 11-year-old daughter would.

Sol, though, guessed her father's true nature from an early age. Being six years older than Mariposa she had witnessed Tomas Ceto's cruelty as he worked his way up the Mexican underworld. Sol had no problem with it: her dad was clearly a big cheese, a kingpin, a legend, did whatever it took to stay on top, however much blood he had to spill.

I would do anything for Dad, thought Sol, playing with her hair in the limo's wing mirror, anything at all. After all she was supposed to be the 'Sun', but Mariposa outshone her every time and this burnt at Sol's proud heart.

*

"That was the best party ever, hey Sol?" said Mariposa, trying to cheer up her sister. "How about that clown! And that piñata we smashed and all those sweets flew out! And that DVD of my new horse at Papi's ranch!"

Mariposa paused. She realized she had said too much. "I'm sure Papi will do something great for your birthday too, Sol…"

"Yeah, right little sister," Sol spat under her breath so their father, who was on his cell phone as usual, wouldn't hear. "What did I get given by Papi at your age - a donkey!" Sol flicked back her fringe. "Just great, hey? You get a prize stallion and I get Shrek's best mate."

Mariposa looked stung by Sol's words. She was still a girl with flowers in her hair, while Sol, 17 now, was a young woman, with a fiery sun tattooed on both her shoulders. They were worlds apart, these sisters. Sol couldn't wait for Mariposa to learn the truth about her 'Papi'. That would smash her silly, Cinderella smile.

Oh yes, Sol told herself, as they passed the huge, marble Bellas Artes palace; it was she who was 'The Sun Queen', her father's true heir. She had the guts for it, the fire in her veins. She was the one who would shine. Mariposa was just a Little Butterfly, her wings too fragile. When things heated up she would be frazzled from the face of the earth.

The limo pulled up at a traffic light. A street boy, no older than Mariposa, started washing the windscreen, squirting foamy water from a plastic bottle over the glass. The boy was caked in dirt and sweat, his face shaded by a baseball cap.

"*Quítate, chico loco,*" shouted Sol, as the boy scrubbed the windscreen. "Go away, crazy boy." She bashed her hand on the windscreen as if swatting a fly.

"Don't be so cruel, Sol," begged Mariposa. "He's only trying to make some money. What's wrong with that?"

Mariposa reached over and pressed the switch to open her window. The heat and smells of the city swirled inside – frying meat from the street stalls, diesel fumes, a whiff of perfume. Music from the truck behind blasted into the sticky evening air. Mariposa grabbed some sweets from her pocket and held them out to the boy.

"*Aquí amigo. Son para ti,*" she called out. "Here friend. For you."

Tomas Ceto, still distracted by his phone call, looked up. His eyes bulged.

"Shut that window now, Mariposa!" he commanded. He leaned over and shoved the startled street boy away. "Don't you know how dangerous that is? I've told you a thousand times, anyone could see us…"

"But why, Papi? All my friends' parents allow it…"

"Your friends' parents, my love, are not Tomas Ceto!" The drug lord puffed himself up and lurched for the window control as Mariposa playfully fended him off.

Just then a motorcyclist dressed in a suede jacket and a red bandana thrummed up beside the limo. He sported sunglasses and shiny, swept-back hair so stiff with gel it looked like a helmet. He flashed Mariposa a movie star smile, his teeth a brilliant white. Mariposa grinned back.

"¡Hola guapa!" said the biker, pushing aside the street boy once again. "Hello beautiful!"

He blew Mariposa a kiss through the open window. "What an angel you are! What a treasure! You must make your Papi very proud!" His voice purred: "Such a proud, proud… TOAD!"

And then, quick as a flash, the biker's smile vanished, his face hard and intense. He unzipped his jacket and ripped out a sawn-off shotgun. Tomas Ceto gasped, snapped shut his phone and pulled Mariposa towards him while Señor Rodríguez, wrestling with the steering wheel, grabbed for his pistol in the glove compartment.

The limo's tires screeched as it swerved across the highway missing a loaded grocery truck by a whisker. Watermelons flew in the air, one bursting on the limo's windscreen, purple juice everywhere. Sol screamed, her hands over her face.

The biker's gun fired: a flash of bright white. Señor Rodríguez, now clutching his pistol, fired back but it was too late, the bike roared away, zigzagging fast through the twilight traffic. The driver leaned out of his window and fired off two more bullets at the fleeing gunman, the cracks of his pistol muted by the screams of terrified bystanders. He missed with both shots, cursing under his breath.

The biker roared around a corner near a statue of a bronze angel, its wings winking in the dying light. Within seconds he was out of range, out of sight. Gone.

Señor Rodríguez didn't hang about. He fired up the stalled limo, revved the engine hard and sped off the road onto a supermarket forecourt. A young woman with a shopping trolley dove for cover. The limo skidded, ricocheted off a lamppost and bombed down a maze of narrow streets before pulling over in an alley beneath a mango tree heavy with fruit.

Señor Rodríguez yanked on the hand brake and the big car lurched to a halt. He opened his door, the smell of mangoes all around, police sirens whirring in the distance.

"We need help quick, boss," said Señor Rodriquez, turning to face the back of the limo for the first time since the shooting.

What he saw made him sick: Tomas Ceto held Mariposa slumped in his lap, stroking her cheek. The young girl's body was limp, her face bloody and her lips a deathly blue. Even the marigolds in her hair were flecked with red.

And there was something else. Something Señor Rodríguez had never seen in all his twenty years of service: Tomas Ceto was weeping.

"*Mi mariposita*," whispered the drug lord again and again, kissing the top of his daughter's head, his whole body convulsed with grief. "My Little Butterfly. My Little Butterfly."

"Oh no, no, no…" said Señor Rodríguez, looking away. He could see he was in charge now: *El Sapo* in meltdown, unable to make any decisions. "It's too late for a hospital, boss, we need to go somewhere safe. Somewhere secret. And fast."

In the passenger seat, Sol sat still as a statue, staring ahead, her hands in tight fists as if praying. Señor Rodríguez put his own trembling hands over hers to offer comfort. He was surprised she was not shaking at all.

"I'm so sorry, Sol," said Señor Rodríguez.

A dog howled nearby, breaking the silence. It was a grim, haunting sound, not quite of this world. Sol looked up, shaken out of her trance, and turned to the back seat, inspecting her stricken family.

As Senor Rodriguez watched her, a chill came over him. What he witnessed he would never forget. Sol appeared pale, surprised, but that was not what stood out about her. No, it was something else. Something terrible. Unthinkable.

Sol was looking at her sobbing father and wounded sister and, yes, smiling, she was smiling. Very subtly, very quietly - but she was definitely smiling. The chauffeur watched her, his heart full of dread, as the lonely dog howled on.

"God help you, Sol," Señor Rodríguez whispered, choking on his words. He moved his hands quickly away from hers, as if he was now touching something foul. "Only God can help you now."

A few seconds later he gunned the engine, kissed a crucifix hanging from the dashboard and drove his ruined cargo into the hot, mango-scented night.

PART TWO

Mexico Bound

Craddly Hill, England
5 years later

A firework blasted high above the park. Fzzzzzzzz! Shweeeee! Then a distant Pop! Hal Bradby watched as streams of yellow and blue ripped across the sky. Pancho, bounding beside him, froze, still as a deer.

"It's ok, boy," said Hal. "Just a rocket."

Pancho looked up, shook his coat, and ran on towards Craddly Hill. No one really knew what breed of dog Pancho was: "half Old English Sheepdog, half wolf, three quarters crazy" in Hal's dad's opinion. At the time Hal had pointed out to his Dad, that ½ and ½ and ¾ meant Pancho wasn't one, but almost two dogs. He loved making fun of his father's lousy math.

Hal was on cloud nine as he walked Pancho. His school holidays had just kicked off and even better, tomorrow he was flying to Mexico. Johnny Bradby was a documentary maker and for the first time was taking his restless son with him on his travels. Hal couldn't wait.

Hal's mum, Gillian, had freaked, worried out of her wits by all the news about violence in Mexico. She'd heard about 'a nasty drug lord called Tomas Geto, or Gecko or maybe Cornetto - something like that', who had just escaped from jail.

Johnny told his wife not to fret, he was making a film about a type of rare butterfly and that Mexican butterflies weren't known for smuggling drugs, kidnapping children or even shooting people - at least not the ones he'd filmed before.

Hal's mum still wasn't convinced but at the last minute, thanks to Gina Moreno, Hal got her blessing.

Gina was a school friend of Hal's, a half Mexican, half English girl, who he had met at the chess club. She had an uncle in Mexico who she really wanted to visit in the school holidays but her parents couldn't get time off work. "Go with my dad instead!" blurted Hal. "He can fly with you."

And so, after lots of phone calls between the families, Johnny Bradby agreed to escort the Moreno's adventurous daughter to her uncle's home in the wild Chihuahua Desert before starting work on his butterfly film. Johnny Bradby knew Mexico well having worked there many times and if Gina could go, he told his wife, so could Hal. Gillian Bradby reluctantly agreed.

Gina was 14, the same age as Hal, and like a hundred other boys at Craddly Hill Grammar, Hal would have happily slain dragons for her. Hal also knew Gina was way out of his league. He was a book-loving nerd with a bird's nest of ginger hair, who even his mum called a 'punky scarecrow.' Gina was sassy, drop dead gorgeous and dating JJ Masters, a gym obsessed beefcake, who looked like he could eat Wolverine for breakfast. Oh yes, Gina Moreno, thought Hal. She was so out of this world she may as well live on Pluto.

Tomorrow, though, Hal would travel with her to Mexico. He couldn't believe his spectacular good luck.

*

A second firework banged off, snapping Gina out of Hal's thoughts. Pancho wasn't spooked at all, just kept bounding through the park. Some swallows were dive bombing a pond up ahead, rippling the soupy water.

"Good dog Pancho," shouted Hal. "Steady boy."

Hal was happy none of the fireworks had bothered Pancho, as the poor mutt normally hated them. The first whizz of a Catherine Wheel or hiss of a sparkler and he'd turn into a doggy zombie, heart pounding, eyes rolling and his mouth filled with slobber.

But right now Pancho had an ear infection so Hal doubted he could hear anything, not rockets, not sparklers, not even volcanoes erupting, though Craddly Hill wasn't known for them. But luckiest of all for Pancho, Hal smiled, is that he didn't have to hear his dad playing Mexican cowboy songs that evening.

It was true. His dad played guitar bad enough to make your ears bleed. The last time he sang with his Mexican-themed band, Pancho Villa and the Sombreros, Hal's little sister, Abby, cried her eyes out; Pancho started howling at the moon and Hal's mum said her husband should enter a new competition: "Britain Hasn't Got Any Talent At All."

Hal couldn't help laughing out loud as he recalled his dad's awful music, while Pancho sniffed about under some nearby chestnut trees. The trees smelled weird and sweaty, like they did that time of summer, when their bark got sticky.

OK, so his dad was a lousy musician, Hal thought, while keeping his eye on Pancho, but so what - he was still an ace filmmaker. A few years ago his dad had won a prize for a film he made in Mexico about Pancho Villa, the famous revolutionary who had a big hat, lots of wives and, best of all for Hal, got heroically shot to pieces in an ambush.

"You love that Pancho Villa more than your family, Johnny Bradby!" Hal's mum had joked at the film premiere party. "You name our dog after him, your band after him and play terrible songs about him getting blasted by bullets. Perhaps we should just all move to Mexico."

Hal's dad had laughed so much that champagne came out of his nose. Oh, his parents, Hal loved them to pieces, but they were beyond embarrassing some-times. With dogs, though, you couldn't go wrong, could you?

Hal looked round and whistled for Pancho, who was now rolling in a patch of nettles beyond the pond. Hal realized he was really going to miss his hairy friend on his Mexican travels.

Lost in the Rain

A car horn honked up ahead. Hal and Pancho were on the home stretch now, striding through the playground near the park entrance. Hal didn't want to be late home as Gina was coming to dinner, then sleeping over before they flew to Mexico City the following morning.

He grabbed hold of Pancho's collar, fumbling in his pocket for the dog lead. Judging by the distant thrum of traffic beyond the park gates, the road was busy.

A pigeon crash-landed on an overhead branch. The pigeon's friends roosting in the same spot were restless. *Coo, coo, keke, coo, coo.*

"*Coo, coo, keke, coo, coo*", to you too, you fat pidges," Hal called up at them.

And then it came, the third firework: FFFZZSHHHH! Really close. And the fourth: FFFZZSHHHH! Closer. And then Hal lost count: FZZZ! SCWHEE! BANG! All around them the pigeons scattered, their wings beating like fury. Pancho ripped free of Hal's grip and shot off up Craddly Hill, his long tail vanishing into the dusk.

Hal bellowed after him but Pancho was scared out of his wits, gaining speed all the time.

"Panchoooo."

When Pancho reached the top of the hill, there was a pause in the banging, and he stopped, peering back at Hal for two or three seconds. "Good boy," Hal whispered, his guts flooding with relief. Then once more – FZZZ! SWEEE! BANG! He was gone.

"Panchoooo!"

By the time Hal reached the wooden bench near the hilltop, he was gasping and sweat-soaked. He leaned against a tree, its bark tattooed with graffiti. Pancho was nowhere to be seen.

The sun, now a tiny red marble, ducked under the horizon taking most of day's warmth and light with it. The suburbs glimmered in the distance. Hal needed help – and fast. He punched his mobile's speed dial.

"Dad? Yes, listen! Pancho's run off. I've lost him. There were fireworks…"

"Why wasn't he on a leash, Hal? asked Johnny Bradby. He sounded angry. "And why are you out so late? We're going to Mexico first thing in the morning!"

"It's summer, Dad, still just about light." Hal said. "I didn't expect any fireworks before dark." Silence. "I'm sorry, but please, we have to find him. Pancho never just runs off."

Johnny Bradby's tone softened. It would be OK, he said. Pancho would be home in no time and they'd make it to Mexico just fine. He told Hal he was going to team up with Harry Brackenberry, the Bradby's neighbor, who loved Pancho almost as much as Hal did.

All the family called Mr Brackenberry 'Mr B'. Well, all except Hal's mum. She called him Flasher Harry because he drank too much cider at a party once and peed on her rose garden. She said Mr B was lonely since his wife had left him last year so she let him take Pancho for walks now and then.

Johnny Bradby and Mr B arrived at the park ten minutes later, Mr B chewing on a donut. Mr B was quite old, used to be in the navy – 'a commander, like James Bond' he'd told Hal once. He didn't look much like 007 tonight. He was pot bellied, pink in the face and wearing a pair of rubber rain boots splattered in mud.

It was almost dark now and had started to drizzle. Hal looked up and groaned. He realized he didn't have any rain gear, just a lousy pair of trainers and a Manchester United T-shirt. Thankfully his dad had brought him a spare coat and a jersey.

"OK, let's get going," said Mr B. "No time to waste, hey Halford." Mr B was the only person to call Hal by his full name.

The three of them spread out in a line and marched down the hill towards the far side of the park. "Pancho! Come on boy!" shouted Hal's dad. "Ahoy Panchoooo," yodelled Mr B. Hal felt too upset to shout anything, but whistled every now and then.

The rain got worse: louder, stronger, ripping into the soggy earth. As Hal could hardly hear the others, he doubted Pancho could either. *Stay safe Pancho*, Hal prayed, *find your way home*. He imagined his pet run over, wounded and bloody in a ditch somewhere…

At the bottom of the hill, the three dog searchers all joined up.

"We must keep going!" yelled Hal. "We have to find Pancho!"

"Steady, tiger," Johnny Bradby put an arm over his son's shoulder. "This really is grim weather. We won't find Pancho till it's blown over."

"Your dad's right, Halford," said Mr B. "Sorry, old man." *Old man*, Hal thought, *I'm about 100 years younger than you!* Mr B pointed at Hal's clothes. "Besides you're drenched."

Hal looked in horror at Mr B, then his dad. How could they stop searching when Pancho was somewhere out there on this dreadful night? So much for Mr B. He was supposed to be a commander, a regular 007. James Bond usually saves the world, Hal fumed. Mr B, the useless cider guts, couldn't even track down a hairy, rocket-spooked mongrel.

Johnny Bradby held out his arms and gave his son a damp hug. Hal breathed in his father's fleece. It smelt of rain, cigarette smoke and home, and Hal wanted to cry. What a fool he was losing his dog in the worst rainstorm since Noah.

Pancho was out there somewhere, alone and afraid, and it was all his fault.

How could he possibly go to Mexico now?

*

"Hal!" A hazy figure appeared in the distance, waving frantically from the top of Craddly Hill. "Hal! Mr Bradby! It's Gina. I've got Pancho!"

Gina was holding Pancho's collar, but when the big hound saw Hal, he broke free, sprinting across the park then jumped up, knocking Hal clean over.

Hal's stomach did about 17 somersaults for joy. It felt like his heart had given his ribs a massive high five. Laughing with relief, he grabbed Pancho and held him close.

"Where were you, you stupid mutt?' said Hal, plunging his face into his dog's soaking mane.

"I saw him crossing the High Street," said Gina, catching her breath back. She had a rucksack on her back, all ready for Mexico, her pretty face dewy with rain.

"Pancho stands out a mile, so I just grabbed him." Gina shrugged her shoulders. " I was on my way to your house anyway, so I called your mum. She told me you were in the park."

"You saved the day, Gina, you're a star," blurted Hal, realizing immediately afterwards that he sounded like a total muppet.

Gina laughed a friendly, 'it was my pleasure' kind of laugh and stroked Pancho's ears, kissing the soggy hound on his nose while telling him: "you gorgeous boy."

"What I'd give to swap places with you now, you dopey pooch," Hal thought to himself.

Ok, that's it, he decided there and then, Gina Moreno was officially his dream girl. Even better, tomorrow she would be miles from JJ Masters, that dozy great, six-packed, oatmeal-for-brains doofus. Oh yes, instead she would be sitting on a Mexico bound plane with him, Halford George Fitzroy Bradby, her punky-fringed, proud-to-be-ginger, scarecrow in shining armor.

Once safely home, Hal's little sister, Abby, dashed over to greet Pancho in her *Finding Nemo* pyjamas. "Pancho Lalapants," she screamed with delight, hanging onto her lost pet's neck.

"Pancho Lalapants?" asked Gina.

"You can get away with names like that when you are four-years-old," joked Hal, giving Abby's ponytail a tug.

Pancho was spoiled rotten that night. Abby fed him about 3000 Choc Drops, Mr B gave him a squeaky bone, Gina tied a Mexican flag around his tail and Hal's mum allowed him up on the sofa while they all watched *Britain's Got Talent*. Johnny Bradby moaned about the useless singers and how one day *Pancho Villa and the Sombreros* would add 'a touch of Mexican class' to the show, until his wife stuffed a cushion in his mouth, and everyone collapsed in laughter.

After dinner, Gina and Hal did some last minute packing before returning to the living room. Hal's mum had gone to bed but Johnny Bradby was glued to the TV news.

On the screen was a photo of a Mexican criminal: Tomas Ceto. Hal studied the picture. He looked like a big fat man with big bug eyes and a big droopy moustache. He also looked like big trouble.

"Drug lord, Tomas Ceto, escaped from his prison cell in Mexico City last week," read the stern-voiced reporter.

"Ceto, one of Mexico's most violent gangsters, was whisked away in a helicopter after smuggling himself out of a high security jail in a laundry basket. Two of Ceto's men and one policeman were killed in a shootout during the escape.

Known as 'El Sapo' or 'The Toad', Ceto, has built up a huge fortune, mostly through drug smuggling. Mexican police are throwing all their resources into finding this brutal killer, but his whereabouts are still a mystery.

Another photo appeared of a snake-eyed girl with tattoos on her shoulders.

"Since his imprisonment five years ago, Ceto's gang has been led by his eldest daughter, Sol, still in her early twenties, but already thought to be every bit as dangerous as her father.

Another snapshot of a young, pretty girl riding a horse briefly flashed on the screen.

Ceto's youngest daughter, Mariposa, known as "Little Butterfly' vanished, aged 11, after a shooting incident in the Mexican capital. She has not been seen since...

"Ok, you two, off to bed now," said Johnny Bradby, clapping his hands. "Let's not worry about all this. We've as much chance of bumping into Tomas Ceto in Mexico as having tea with Lady Gaga." He looked at his watch. "I'm setting my alarm for 6. Let's all get some sleep."

Having given Gina his room, Hal crashed out on the sofa and cuddled up with Pancho. As he grabbed the TV control, Tomas Ceto's photo appeared one more time - a shot of the drug lord holding hands with a young girl with marigolds in her hair. It had clearly been taken many years ago. They both looked very happy.

"Tomas Ceto can't be that bad, hey Pancho," said Hal, studying the photo.

He prodded the zapper once more and, in a flash, Tomas Ceto and the Little Butterfly were gone. They were replaced by a *Britain's Got Talent* hopeful, a chubby, droopy-faced man with a ponytail called Barry. Barry was being told by Simon Cowell that his singing sounded worse than "a walrus being harpooned - and that's being unfair on the walrus."

Hal secretly prayed his dad never got anywhere near Simon Cowell. A whole choir of Barrys or even a colony of harpooned walruses would sound like the sweetest music on earth compared to *Pancho Villa and the Sombreros.*

Snow from the Moon

Mexico City spread out below them, a mass of shimmering white lights. It was so big, just looking down at it from the plane's window made Hal's blood fizz.

"What a view," he whispered to Gina. She was quiet, in awe of the spectacle below.

It was bright enough to believe that the Milky Way had collapsed and crash-landed directly under them. Everything seemed on a topsy-turvy scale. The mountains fringing the city were huge but from up in the air Hal thought they looked tiny, dwarfed by the shining monster beneath them: perhaps the biggest city on earth, his dad had told him.

"Just like Craddly Hill, hey Hal?" said Johnny Bradby, watching his son's face.

"Identical, Dad. Well, apart from 20 million more people."

"And maybe a few more Mexican restaurants," said Gina.

This was the first time Hal had flown and he loved it. The adrenalin rush at take off; the map of the plane's location and speed (578 miles an hour!); the tiny screen with every TV show under the sun (including Tomas Ceto's ugly mug appearing on a news flash), the air crew always on call…What more could he want? Well, except the most beautiful girl in Craddly Hill sitting next to him.

For all the excitement, though, Hal had found it tough saying goodbye to his mum, Abby and Pancho. Apart from a school camping weekend near Stonehenge he'd spent very little time away from home.

Hal's mum had been full of tears at the airport and clung onto Hal like she'd never see him again. Hal joked with Gina that his mum had cried even more than at the end of her favorite film, *Titanic*, when Kate Winslet says: "I'll never let go, Jack", even though she does let go and Leonardo di Caprio goes plunging to the bottom of the ocean like a high-speed, ice-faced torpedo!

Neither Abby nor Pancho really grasped that Hal and his dad were leaving, but Hal knew they'd be fine: after all, it was only for a month.

The plan was that they'd spend a night in Mexico City, before flying up to meet Gina's uncle in Ciudad Juárez, a Tex-Mex border town on the fringes of the Chihuahua Desert. They would stay there a while then Hal would join his dad filming butterflies in the jungles of southern Mexico.

"We're landing now," said Johnny Bradby, peering down. "This chewing gum might help." He handed Hal and Gina a strip each. "Your mum hates landings, Hal. Last time we flew she swallowed her gum and threw up on my lap."

"Nice one, Dad. Thanks for sharing."

An hour later they were in a red and gold taxi, driving through downtown Mexico City. Hal could hardly believe it. *Woohoo! Mexico!* The area around the airport had looked chewed up, but now they were speeding past a statue of a bronze angel lit up in the night sky. Soon they arrived at a massive square surrounded by ancient, dimly lit buildings.

"This square's called the Zócalo," said Hal's dad, as they rumbled over the cobbles. "The heart of Mexico City."

They checked into the top floor of a hotel a few minutes walk from the city center. The three-bed room was cozy with orange walls and pictures of tropical birds. It was already late so they unpacked, took turns in the bathroom, and soon all fell into a deep sleep, not even the nearby cathedral bells chiming midnight waking them.

Nor did they hear another sound - the whoosh of Tomas Ceto's private jet flying overhead. From the safety of their room they remained blissfully unaware that *El Sapo*, the newly escaped drug lord and Sol, his fierce-hearted daughter, were zooming towards Ciudad Juárez – Gina Moreno's uncle's home.

*

Johnny Bradby rose early, woke Hal and Gina, and took them out for breakfast at a nearby street stall. They crouched on wooden stools on the pavement, while a man in a white suit played to them on his violin. Hal's dad ordered them all *huevos revueltos* – scrambled eggs – and a mango milkshake.

After breakfast, they wandered around the Zócalo. As they took photos a gypsy woman approached Johnny Bradby with a sign: 'MIRACLE PILLS: CURE BALDNESS!" Hal's dad scratched at his receding hair just to make sure it was still there. "Don't worry Dad," said Hal, laughing. "You're better off than Mr B, he's bald as an egg. Let's buy him a bucket full."

From the Zócalo they lit a candle in the cathedral, watched a street performer breathing fire and drank *horchata* – a sweet, milky drink made from rice– before Johnny Bradby hailed a passing mini-bus.

"Where are we going now?" Hal asked, jumping in, Gina in tow.

"To see my favorite view in Mexico." Johnny Bradby replied, scratching his beard. "Let's get some fresh air."

Soon they were weaving out of the congested city. The bus driver was squinting like a mole. This was hardly surprising as his wind screen was full of all sorts of stuff – an air freshener shaped like a Smurf, several crucifixes, a big picture of his wife and children and dozens of other photos including The Virgin Mary, Selena Gómez, Elvis and a load of Mexican football players Hal didn't know.

"How can he see out of that windscreen?" whispered Hal.

"From the way he's swerving about I don't think he can," said Gina. She laughed and made a sign of the cross on her chest.

Hal fell asleep for a bit. When he woke, Gina had her head on his shoulder and they were travelling through lush, rolling countryside. Oh, if you could see us now, JJ Masters, you great meathead, Hal thought happily, you'd really get your gym shorts in a twist.

The road became even windier and they finally pulled up under a palm tree at a village gas station.

"This is it," said Hal's dad, jumping out of the bus.

Johnny Bradby strutted off like a bionic penguin, as Hal and Gina dashed after him. They barged their way through the bustling village square and passed a white chapel, its door smothered in red flowers. In the distance Hal could see the rocky hills they were going to climb.

On the way Mexican villagers tried to flog them everything from T-shirts to bows and arrows. A woman with earrings the size of ping-pong balls was reading palms and an elderly man with a ponytail was painting a cartoon of a couple of tourists.

At the bottom of the hill, Hal's dad bought a hunk of watermelon to snack on while they climbed. As they waited for him, Hal and Gina saw a tiny green hummingbird flash by.

The climb was easy at first, up several flights of stone steps. These soon faded onto a steep, dirt path full of tree roots and boulders. They all kept a good, steady pace, shaded by the dense vegetation. Occasionally they passed other walkers slogging their way up.

An hour later they reached the peak – a small, Aztec pyramid carved with serpents and scary-looking ancient Gods. As Hal and Gina collapsed in a heap, gulping at their water bottles, Hal's dad explained that the Aztec people, who lived at this spot hundreds of years ago, were very civilized, way ahead of their time in architecture, math and medicine.

"All I remember from school history lessons," said Hal, "was that the Aztecs ripped out thousands of human hearts, including women's and children's." Hal pretended to stab Gina in the chest. "Did it as a sacrifice to feed human blood to the sun."

"Gross," said Gina, pulling a face. "That doesn't sound very civilized at all! More like something Tomas Ceto would do."

"Alright, alright, you two," said Johnny Bradby. "Let's not dwell on Mexico's violence then or now." He pointed ahead. "Look at this instead…"

The view of the mountains below was striking but what was really cool, Hal decided, were the eagles above them riding the thermals. He lay back against the pyramid with Gina and together they watched the graceful birds swooping and gliding. Hal didn't know if he'd ever felt quite so happy.

After a while Hal's dad stood up, fired off some photos and put a cigarette in his mouth.

"I know I shouldn't," he said, flicking open his lighter. "Smoking's a foul habit and I wish I'd never started. But hey, it's my first ciggie in weeks." He grinned "And this is a special occasion. Tomorrow we're off to Ciudad Juárez. But today is free, just you two and me."

Johnny Bradby dragged deep on the cigarette and blew up a smoke ring. He looked very chilled.

"You know something," he said, his eyes on Hal and Gina. "When you travel, you have moments where you wonder what on earth you are doing. When you'd much rather be home." He paused, wiping the sweat from his brow.

"But there are other times when you're so happy, you wouldn't want to be any-where else." He exhaled some smoke. "In the zone, in other words."

"In the zone? Sounds a bit deep, Dad."

"It's a tough one to describe," Hal's father furrowed his brow, like he sometimes did when he played guitar.

"I was filming in Java once, an island in Indonesia. Lovely place." Johnny Bradby smiled at the memory. "They have an expression there 'Snow From The Moon'. Beautiful hey?"

"Really beautiful," agreed Gina.

"But not as beautiful as you, Gina Moreno," Hal almost said, but was delighted his inner cheesy comment detector stopped him just in time.

"Anyway," said Johnny Bradby. "Snow from the moon. It means something so rare and wonderful, it's almost impossible to imagine." He laughed. "Hey, I'm getting really deep now, aren't I?"

"Don't worry, Professor Einstein. We're just about following you."

"Anyway," he added, grabbing Hal and Gina's shoulders. "What I mean, is that this, right here, right now, is Snow From The Moon. You two, me, an ancient pyramid, mountains, fresh air, eagles flying above us…"

"Don't forget the cigarette."

Hal's dad laughed and exhaled some smoke. "Don't tell, mum, will you! It's a one off, I promise. Back to that horrible fake plastic one tomorrow."

As they walked back down the steps of the pyramid, clothes damp with sweat, Hal noticed something under his feet: a newspaper someone had left on the track. A familiar face, with a big moustache, stared out from the front page as it rippled in the breeze. Hal picked it up.

TOMAS CETO SPOTTED IN CIUDAD JUÁREZ
Has drug lord returned to his hometown?
By Enrique González

"Gina," Hal said, slowly reading the story. "Isn't Ciudad Juárez where your uncle lives?"

Miracles in Hell

Hal felt tense within minutes of landing in Ciudad Juárez, the whole place was on edge, the air electric.

The airport was overflowing with police in body armor and black helmets. Most had machine guns, dangling casual as tennis rackets from their shoulders, and one or two had hand grenades, the size of oranges, in their belts. Tomas Ceto and Sol were once again splashed all over the paper headlines.

WHERE IS THE TOAD?
ESCAPED DRUG LORD IN MYSTERY HIDEAWAY!

The three new arrivals were thoroughly frisked at the security gate and asked to empty their bags.

"The only drugs they'll find on me," whispered Johnny Bradby, as a policeman inspected a pair of his boxer shorts. "Are some cod liver oil pills for my bad back."

Gina's uncle, Antonio, had been delayed, so to kill time they all ate a ham and egg burrito in the airport cafe. It was still very early, the sun not fully up, the sky bathed in a purple glow.

As he chewed his breakfast, Hal felt uneasy. He had a lot of new info to take on board. Neither his dad nor Gina had been very honest with him over the last couple of days. In fact, they had been keeping him totally in the dark.

On the short flight north from Mexico City, Gina had revealed all.

She did have a Mexican uncle: at least that much was true. What she hadn't told Hal, though, was that he was known as The Pastor and ran a charity for drug addicts called *Miracles in Hell* in one of Mexico's roughest, driest, remotest spots. Gina was going to help out there.

As for Hal's dad, yes, it was true he was going to make a documentary about Mexican butterflies but first up he was going to make a film about The Pastor. He wanted Hal to volunteer with Gina at *Miracles in Hell* while the filming took place.

But, worst of all, Hal now realized, neither Gina nor his dad had been at all truthful about Ciudad Juárez.

"So Ciudad Juárez is pretty dangerous?" said Hal, gesturing out of the airport window at a squad of soldiers marching by.

"Mmm, to be honest," said his dad, breezily, "it's one of the most dangerous cities in the world right now."

"Oh, nice Dad, thanks for telling me that – now we are **HERE**!"

"Yes, your dad's right," said Gina, all matter of fact. "Uncle Antonio told me that more people died in Mexico over the last few years than in the big wars in Afghanistan and Iraq put together."

She shrugged her shoulders. "I don't understand it really, but basically Mexico supplies America drugs, America supplies Mexico guns, and being on the border here Ciudad Juárez is bang in the middle of it all."

"This just gets better and better," thought Hal.

"It'll be even worse with Tomas Ceto here," added his dad, still chirpy as ever. "Now he'll fight for power with Pretty Boy Sánchez, the current chief gangster here."

Johnny Bradby smiled at Hal, dragging on his fake plastic cigarette as if his life depended on it. "Sorry for not telling you earlier, son, but we couldn't let mum know, she'd have a fit. Gina and I were worried you'd be put off coming. But I know we'll be fine." He slapped Hal's back, "it'll be a great experience for you."

"I was here last year too," said Gina. "But I promised your dad I wouldn't tell you until the right moment."

"You've been here before!" blurted Hal. "Wasn't it super scary?

"No, not really." Gina coolly chewed on her burrito. "I never even heard a gunshot. Yes, there was lots of terrible news in the papers. Shootings, kidnaps and things, but my uncle's charity is ten miles out of town in the Chihuahua Desert. We'll all be safe there."

"Wow, you are seriously brave, Gina," said Hal, inwardly slapping himself for sounding like a 7-year-old girl.

"Not at all," said Gina. "I just come here for Uncle Antonio. He's a bit nuts but he's totally amazing. He helps all the people in the city nobody else wants - the homeless, the druggies and the loonies." She rolled her eyes at Hal and put on a wacky voice. "They are part of The Pastor's big, craaaaazy family. I just like helping out."

"That's amazing!" Hal said, but he was actually thinking: "That's nuts!"

"Oh well," Hal added, trying not to sound too fazed, "sounds like you two have got my life all sorted."

Outside, another tank-like vehicle rumbled by, followed by some armed heavies on motorbikes.

"I'm going to call your uncle, Gina, see what's holding him up," said Johnny Bradby.

He pulled out his cell phone. It was an old model with gigantic buttons. Hal shook his head.

"Dad, I swear that's the only phone still visible from space!" he teased. "I hope that's not our emergency backup. That ring tone must have been around at the time of the Aztecs. Or even Julius Caesar!"

"Oh, long before then, son," said Johnny Bradby, winking at Gina. "I'm old school. I talk with my mouth, not my thumbs like you two…"

Just as Johnny Bradby was about to dial his prehistoric phone, The Pastor ran through the arrivals hall, arms waving all over the place like an excited football referee.

"Gina! Gina! Over here!

He was a great big bear of a man, wearing a purple poncho. In his hand was a walking stick even taller than him. He had a wild grin on his face.

Wow, thought Hal, he certainly stands out from the crowd.

Gina ran up to The Pastor, who dropped his stick and lifted her clean off the ground, giving her a long hug.

"Hola, mi estrellita," he roared. "Hello, my little star. So good to see you again. And this must be…" The Pastor held out his hand to Johnny Bradby. "Hal's dad, and here we have…" he shifted his hand, "young Hal. Great to see you, and thank you for bringing my lion-hearted niece here."

"Our pleasure," said Johnny Bradby.

The Pastor grabbed Gina's backpack and hefted it on to his giant shoulders. "OK, my friends," he said, waving everyone forward. "Let's all go to the madhouse!"

Together they walked out to the airport car park, dazzled by the sun's laser-bright light.

The Pastor's battered, red pick-up truck, like its owner, also stood out from the crowd. It had **MILAGROS EN EL INFIERNO – MIRACLES IN HELL –** written on the side and a set of bullhorns prodding out of the car hood. Hal volunteered to sit in the back so the others could fit in the front cab.

"That's good of you, Hal," said The Pastor. "But cover up – we are in the desert now, this sun can burn your butt off. And one more thing," he pointed inside the truck, "I have a new friend."

The Pastor opened the passenger door and a dog leapt out, its tail wagging furiously. It was a turbo-charged mongrel with a gold coat, one eye dark, one eye blue and covered in dust.

"I found him on the side of the road just now," said The Pastor. "There's so many half-starved mutts in Juárez." He shrugged his shoulders. "All my crazy folks at the charity love them."

The dog leapt up on Hal, pawing at his T-shirt.

"I think he likes you Hal," said The Pastor. "Why don't you look after him? That would be a real help. What do you want to call him?"

"Pancho!" Hal, Gina and Johnny Bradby all said the word at once and started to laugh.

"Good name," agreed The Pastor. "Pancho it is then!"

While the others got in the front of the truck, Hal picked up Pancho and plonked him in the boot before jumping in himself. They nestled down on a couple of beanbags by the truck's tailgate.

Before they headed off another couple of volunteers – a teenage girl and an older man – appeared. They were both laden down with groceries. Hal helped them load the bags as they joined him in the back of the truck.

"Beautiful sunrise," said Hal, gesturing to the purplish sky. "I'm Hal, by the way."

Neither of them said a word. Bit rude, thought Hal. What's their problem? Maybe they don't speak any English – but most people living on the Tex-Mex border spoke at least a bit. Why were they both treating him like dirt?

Hal glanced up at the girl. She had a butterfly tattooed on both her shoulders and a bracelet engraved with the word *Sweet Pea*. She was probably only in her mid-teens but her face was a bit roughed up. Her forehead and left cheek looked liked they'd been lightly scarred and one of her eyes was slightly out of sync with the other. She had her frizzy hair tied back and a permanent scowl.

Next to her was the hulk-like, older man. He had a skinhead haircut and a big wart on his nose that looked like a piece of chewing gum that had been spat out.

Hal was glad he had Pancho with him; these two were pretty grim company.

*

As it was still early the road to *Miracles in Hell* was almost deserted. Apart from the slums on the edge of the city there was nothing but miles of sand, scrappy trees and the odd 'blink and you miss it' ranch.

All was silent apart from The Pastor singing along to a Mexican cowboy song on the radio as he drove. The breeze felt good and Hal started to nod off. After a few minutes he woke up with a start.

"Keep your dog under control!" shouted the scowly-faced girl, smacking Pancho on the head.

Pancho had clearly jumped up on her. Bad idea. The smacked hound now skulked back to Hal, tail between his legs.

"You have no idea do you, you idiot," added Scowly Girl. "Just come to Mexico for a few days and think you own the place! You don't even know how to look after youself, let alone your crazy dog".

Hal was gobsmacked. He'd never even seen this girl before today, let alone spoken to her. She sounded so angry and full of hate. Hal grabbed Pancho. "Here boy, it's ok. You didn't mean any harm did you?"

The older volunteer with the warty nose gave Hal a sinister glare. Hal noticed he also had a pistol holstered to his hip. His guts churned. Wart Nose and Scowly Face were a seriously scary pair. He decided he would keep his distance from now on.

Soon after, the truck pulled up outside a concrete building shaped like a giant breezeblock. Across it, in big, white letters, was written:

ALBERGUE PARA PERSONAS CON PROBLEMAS DE SALUD MENTAL

"What does that mean?" Hal asked The Pastor, after they'd all got out of the truck.

"Home for Crazy People," replied Uncle Antonio, winking. "And that includes me! Welcome aboard."

Wart Face and Scowly Girl scuttled off with the shopping while the three newcomers followed The Pastor. The landscape around them was all sand and rock apart from a few tough looking trees called *mesquites*, which, according to Gina, were able to survive on hardly any water.

"I need to talk to your dad about the documentary he's making here, Hal," said The Pastor, as they reached the main gate. "Why don't you two youngsters go clean up and join us for lunch." He grabbed Hal's shoulder. "We're eating *menudo*, young man! You're in for a treat!"

"What's this *menudo*?" Hal asked Gina, as they peeled away from the adults.

"Ah, good old *menudo*," said Gina. "It's like a brown soup full of random cow parts, mostly intestines."

"Wow," said Hal. "I hope it tastes better than it sounds."

"Oh no way, trust me, whatever you're thinking, it's worse."

They walked through the gate into a large, dusty courtyard. The first thing that Hal noticed were the blankets everywhere – bright squares of red, blue, green and yellow – hanging in every available space from washing lines, balconies and mesquite trees.

Then the smell hit him: a sour stink, like old milk or sweaty clothes.

"These blankets are washed every day," Gina told Hal, seeing him gawp. "They have to be, you see, well, it's like, um..."

"Like what?" Hal asked. "Come on spit it out…"

"Well, some people here are ex-gang members and drug addicts." Gina paused and then whispered: "Can't control their pee and poo."

"Eww," said Hal, wincing.

"One of your jobs will be cleaning them," Gina prodded him playfully in the ribs. "Don't worry, you'll soon get used to it. " She waved her hand. "I'll go and get scrubbed up. See you later for some *menudo*."

"Cow gut soup, you mean," said Hal. "Can't wait!"

Human Junkyard

After showering Hal made his way to lunch. En route to the dining area he met with his first *Miracles in Hell* challenge.

A woman wrapped in a pink blanket with wild, curly hair ran up and pulled on his arm. She was groaning, like she wanted to talk but couldn't. Spit was coming from the edge of her mouth and she smelled like something rotten. Hal pushed her away in shock.

"Sorry about that, Lupita," Gina said, appearing from the dining area and taking the groaning woman gently by the hand.

"You can meet *him* later." She glared at Hal. "When he's in a *better mood*! Now, how about some lunch, hey Loopy Lou?"

Gina gave Hal a parting 'what do you think you're doing' frown. *Ouch*, he thought, he hadn't made a very promising start at all.

Once other members of The Pastor's 'family' had seen Gina they ran from all corners of the courtyard to welcome her, swarming around her as they joined the lunch line.

The Pastor had warned his 'family' was shocking, Hal thought as he watched Gina deal with them, and he was right! Some of them were crying or laughing or talking to themselves. One old man in a blue sweater was dancing as if being blasted by massive electric shocks. Another young boy, no more than 18, with cuts on his arms, was singing into space.

A heavy, middle-aged lady with a bandage on her head came up to Hal's dad. She looked on the verge of tears and pretty bonkers. Johnny Bradby smiled, spoke to her in Spanish and gave her a hug. Hal couldn't believe how cool his dad was with everyone, as if this was all just a picnic.

Hal felt ashamed at how awkward he felt. True, he spoke good Spanish (top of his class at school thanks to Gina's help), but he hadn't been abroad before and he was only 14. Then he looked at Gina, the same age as him, acting like some sort of hyper-efficient angel.

"Don't panic, Hal." The Pastor appeared by his side, as if reading his thoughts. "This place is a shock I know. It's very basic. We just do our best to help, that's all."

Hal smiled at him, trying to show that he was fine, even though he wasn't. He was scared out of his wits.

"Just give it time." The Pastor put his arm around Hal. "They are simply human beings like you and me. They've just all had really tough lives."

"Sorry, Pastor. This is all just a bit new for me."

 "You're OK, Hal. Just try to be kind." He beamed at Hal and handed him a plastic bowl full of *menudo*. "Here," he said, "a classic Mexican lunch! The chewy bits are the best, the cow's lungs." He let out a wicked laugh, as Hal took a couple of mouthfuls.

"So what do you think?"

Hal chewed on a chunk of cow guts. "Better than I thought," said Hal, pulling a face. "But still the worst thing I've ever tasted in my life."

"Good man, Hal!" The Pastor roared. "You are going to fit right in here."

*

After his first afternoon at *Miracles in Hell*, Hal felt blown apart.

His social life in Craddly Hill revolved around his mum, dad and Abby, and playing around with Pancho and a few schoolmates. That was about it.

At The Pastor's place, he hung out with a very different crowd.

So let's see, thought Hal: well, there was, Jose, an ex-gangster who'd lost his left hand after being stabbed by a rival gang member; Lupita (Loopy Lou), a dancer who had attacked her cheating husband with saucepan, Marianna, a girl of 19 with an illness called schizo-something whose family had thrown her out due to her loony moods and Jorge, an ex-drug smuggler –thought to be one of Tomas Ceto's gang– who'd been shot in the chest (you could see the bullet hole!) and couldn't speak. Then there was Pedro, a gentle, round-faced Down Syndrome boy, whose family couldn't afford to look after him.

But The Pastor was right, Hal decided, as the day went on, it did get better.

Thanks to watching Gina and his dad mingle with everyone, Hal got more confident too.

He got on especially well with Jose, the one-handed guy.

Jose spoke pretty good English. As a young man he'd moved to America where he'd turned into a 'crazy gangster'. Jose told Hal he'd been 'half dead' when he came back to Mexico but The Pastor took him in and he'd now been at *Miracles in Hell* for over 10 years. He was also The Pastor's sidekick, his best friend –his right hand man.

"Well, I couldn't be his left hand man, could I, Hal?" Jose joked, lifting up his left arm stump. Hal thought he was pretty cool.

After lunch, Hal played football with Pedro, the Down Syndrome boy, before helping Jose hang up blankets on the mesquite trees. As always, Pancho followed him everywhere.

*

It wasn't until dusk that Hal joined up with Gina again. She was peeling potatoes for dinner on a chair outside the kitchen. She smiled up at him. Hal was relieved, he seemed to have been forgiven him for his mean treatment of Loopy Lou earlier in the day.

"I see you've been settling in," said Gina, wiping the sweat from her brow, "making friends."

"Yes, I have," said Hal. Then he remembered the two volunteers with the shopping. "Well, except for that girl with the butterfly tattoos and her scary friend who were in the truck with me."

"Uh-oh, sounds like you mean Rosalita," said Gina, looking up from her work. "A surprisingly cute name for such a complete cow!"

"You can't say that!"

"Wanna bet." She smirked. "Sorry, Hal. I know that's harsh, but she's been really rude to me in the past. She loves The Pastor but she's got a big problem with the other volunteers, especially me."

"Me, too, by the looks of it."

"She probably sees you as a *gringo*. A foreigner." Gina flicked a fly away from her face. "It's a word used for Americans, but some Mexicans use it for any white people."

"But you're not a *gringo*," replied Hal. "You're half Mexican!"

"Oh, she sees me as *fresa*. That means strawberry in Spanish. A spoiled little rich girl," Gina laughed. "She's probably right but at least I haven't got a lumberjack sized, great chip on my shoulder." She rose up, draining the bucket of peeled potatoes. "Or a face like a wounded monkey."

"Whoa, Gina, that's cruel." Hal was shocked by Gina's meanness, but he had to admit part of him enjoyed it too. He really hadn't liked the way Rosalita had whacked Pancho. And her wart-nosed companion hadn't been a bundle of laughs either.

"Who's that big guy who's always with her?"

"Oh, you mean Marco the Narco. Complete thug!" Gina paused. "A *narco* is basically a drug dealer if you didn't know."

Hal didn't. Not really the sort of slang you'd hear in downtown Craddly Hill.

Gina explained that Rosalita had supposedly been in a car crash several years ago. The crash had spoiled her looks and her life. Her family had shunned her and she'd gone off the rails. She'd finally fled to The Pastor, having read about him in a Juárez newspaper. Gina thought the story didn't add up but she didn't want to pry. The Pastor had told her Rosalita wasn't her real name.

The big guy, Marco the Narco, was believed to be Rosalita's uncle, Gina continued. Marco used to be a small-time gangster in Juárez and had now gone straight. He'd always doted on Rosalita, and seemed to be the only one of the family who had stuck by her.

"To be fair to Rosalita or whatever her name is," added Gina. "She cleaned herself up really quickly when she met The Pastor. And she's probably the hardest working volunteer here. I feel a bit sorry for her." Gina shrugged and poured the peeled potatoes into a saucepan. "But I've tried to be kind and she's just acted like…well, like a complete cow!"

"Maybe she's jealous," Hal said.

"What, that I get to hang around with you." Gina tickled Hal in the ribs. "While she gets to hang out with creepy old Marco the Narco."

"No, no…" Hal said, blushing, "jealous of your life."

Gina gave Hal a peck on the cheek, looked in his eyes and grabbed the saucepan of potatoes. "Gotta dash, my ginger friend," she said, and shot back into the kitchen." By the way," she turned back, "you did really well this afternoon."

*

59

Soon after, Hal was left sitting in the courtyard with Pancho. "Just you and me then, boy," he said, stroking his new companion's ears, but still lost somewhere in Gina Moreno's eyes.

Hal heard movement and looked up. Rosalita walked by with Marco the Narco, as always, two steps behind her.

"*Hola!*" he said, trying to sound friendly. "Hello!"

Rosalita was wearing a blue singlet, the butterfly tattoos on her shoulders clearly visible. She turned to look at Hal and scowled. If ever a look could curdle milk, Hal decided, Rosalita was your girl. She spat in the sand at his feet. She really was a charmer this one. Marco the Narco, still armed with his pistol, looked over and shrugged, as if to say: *Nothing to do with me, boy.*

"Just keep that dog under control, alright!" Rosalita gestured to Pancho. "And that little girlfriend of yours. She really seems to think she's The Pastor's golden girl.

"Don't talk about Gina like that…"

"I'll talk about her anyway I like."

Rosalita spat again, fired a look harsh enough to turn both Pancho and Hal to stone, and strutted off, Wart Face hot on her heels. Hal felt a bit shaken up. He thought about telling The Pastor but decided not to bother. He'd just stay as far from them both as possible.

*

Later that evening Hal and his dad Skyped home to England from The Pastor's office.

Pancho, the Craddly Hill dog, was so confused seeing Hal with Pancho, the Mexican dog, that he didn't know whether to lick them or bite them. And Abby was equally bewildered, trying to touch the screen, not sure why Hal couldn't just walk out and greet her.

After a while Hal left to join Gina on the courtyard balcony. He wanted to give his Dad some time on his own with his mum. He sensed his mum was still a little freaked out about them being in Mexico, especially with Tomas Ceto on the news every day. If his mum knew they were all in Ciudad Juárez hanging out with narcos and nutters she'd have a fit.

The balcony was warm in the late afternoon sun. Gina and Hal sat on swing chairs drinking papaya juice and gossiping about home, school and Craddly Hill. A police siren wailed far away, somewhere in Ciudad Juárez.

At times the two teenagers both fell silent and looked out across towards El Paso, Ciudad Juárez's sister town on the American side of the border. Running beside it was the Rio Grande, a slim, dirty river, acting as a barrier between Mexico and Texas.

The sunset was playing out its dying moments in a blaze of red. Hal didn't mind the silences with Gina, they felt right somehow.

"Juárez is a rough city," said Gina, breaking the spell. "But you know what, El Paso, just half a mile away in Texas" –she gestured north towards the border–"is one of the safest cities in America, all neat and orderly, unlike the chaos here. Hardly any murders at all. I don't get it. It's like two different worlds."

Gina said the people in El Paso used to visit Ciudad Juárez all the time, but they had almost totally stopped now –terrified by all the bad news on American TV about Mexico and the drug war. This was sad for Juárez, as the two places had been so united before –it was like El Paso had pulled up a drawbridge.

"They are good people in El Paso," said Gina. "Just too scared by all the bad headlines. You can't blame them."

"Oh, well, El Paso sounds a bit boring," Hal said. "No way you'd hang out with Marco the Narco and Butterfly Tattoo Girl out there!"

"That's true," said Gina, laughing.

The last slither of sun sank below the horizon.

"Juárez isn't the most beautiful place in the world," said Gina, staring at the evening sky. "But Uncle Antonio says we get the best sunsets." She smiled. "And for a place with the worst reputation I still think it has some of the best people."

"I agree," said Hal.

They both fell quiet again, just the sound of crickets chirping, or rubbing their legs together (or whatever they did, Hal couldn't remember) to make that strange, chirrupy sound. Time stood still.

"Mamma Mia, Hal!" Gina shot up off her chair, looking at her watch. "Sorry, I'm really late for a meeting with Uncle Antonio. Gotta go." Gina leant over Hal's chair, her face stopping close to his. She smiled and looked at him with her dark, dancing eyes. She gave his hand a squeeze and his cheek a long kiss. "It's good to have you here, Hal."

There was another long pause.

"What about JJ Masters?" croaked Hal, his head spinning. "Wouldn't Mister Muscles blow a bicep if he saw you kissing me."

"Oh that idiot." Gina sniffed and tossed her head in the air. "Saw him smooching with that bimbo, Jackie Styles, at the bus stop the other week."

"I'm sorry to hear that," Hal lied.

"Don't worry." Gina winked, her hair cascading into Hal's face. "I got my mum to drive through a puddle and soak the pair of them!" She gave Hal another kiss on the cheek before dashing off towards the kitchen. "See you tomorrow, Ginger Boy."

Hal didn't reply. He was unable to reply. He was unable to breathe. In fact he thought his heart may have stopped for about 10 seconds. Maybe 10 minutes. He was still able to smile though.

He looked out at El Paso and felt sorry for it. Give me The Pastor's place any day, he thought. Everyone he'd met so far had been super friendly, well, except for Scowly Girl and Wart Face. And so what if it was home to a few ex gang members. More importantly, it was the Mexican home of Gina, Gina Moreno, and that alone, not forgetting the cow gut soup and blow-your-mind sunsets, made it the finest place on earth.

*

Hal's plan to stay away from Scowly Girl and Wart Nose didn't last long.

The following morning Gina took a shopping trip to Juárez and that left Hal with the lovely Rosalita and the charming Marco. "*Whoohoo,* my lucky day!" he thought.

Things got off to a bad start. The three of them began by stripping all the blankets and taking them to the communal wash basins. Pancho followed Hal about everywhere and regularly got death stares from Rosalita. It didn't seem to bother the skinny mongrel much. He just wagged his tail at her, making her even grouchier.

Once they'd finished a couple of hours later, Hal stopped for a juice break in the kitchen, while Pancho rolled in the sand outside. It was a scorching day, lots of flies drowsily buzzing about.

Hal crouched down on a stool, sipping his juice. Something caught his eye, something glinting in the sand in front of him. Hal picked it up and studied it: a butterfly made of shiny, orange stone. Tied around it was a thin leather strap that had clearly snapped. Hal polished the butterfly on his shorts, deciding he would hand it over to The Pastor. It was a beautiful necklace engraved with the words *MARIPOSITA*.

"Give that back," snapped Rosalita behind him, snatching the butterfly from his hand. "I've been looking everywhere for it. My Papi gave it to me years ago. It's mine, nothing to do with you."

"Er, sorry, just having a quick look. I found it in the sand." Hal shrugged. "We're cool. No worries."

63

"We're cool, no worries," Rosalita mocked his voice, holding the butterfly to her chest. "You should be working, you idiot, not lounging around. We're serving tea and biscuits any minute."

"Yes, Your Majesty," Hal said, under his breath.

Hal joined Rosalita and Marco in the courtyard where The Pastor, in his purple poncho, was filling mugs with tea from an urn while Jose was doling out biscuits with his good arm.

Hal helped hand around biscuits to various family members, including Loopy Lou, the saucepan attacker woman, who was in a very good mood. She had found a dead rattlesnake and wrapped its skin around her neck, proudly displaying it to everyone, like a supermodel with a scarf.

Hal noticed Rosalita was with Jorge, the bullet in the chest guy, who was slumped in his wheelchair in the shade. She was frothing Jorge's face with foam, ready to shave him. She worked carefully, chatting away, and making Jorge smile. Hal noticed Rosalita was always kind with the most messed up members of the family –Jorge, Loopy Lou– even if she was a witch to everyone else.

Once all the biscuits had been eaten Hal sat with The Pastor and Jose under a mesquite tree. He continued watching Rosalita shaving Jorge.

"Rosalita been giving you a hard time, buddy?" asked The Pastor. Hal was impressed The Pastor always seemed to know what he was thinking.

"Not really," said Hal, but his face clearly said something else.

"Be honest with me."

"Ok, yes. Yes, she has!" Hal laughed. "A really hard time!"

"Don't worry, she does it to all the volunteers," said The Pastor. "She has her demons our Rosi." He smiled. "She's actually got a good heart but hidden very well."

The Pastor said that every member of his 'family' was messed up before they came. Many were drug addicts or gang members, lost or angry or just plain mad.

Some recovered, some didn't, but they were all offered help, whatever their demons. Some had family who visited but most were completely alone in the world.

"You should have seen me when I got here," said Jose, sipping on his tea. "I had smoked, eaten, sniffed and drunk just about every illegal substance in the world." He grabbed Hal's arm as he said this. "Please promise me you will never, ever take any drugs, Hal. I was a hopeless addict, a pathetic case, would do anything for my next fix, even rob my own mother. I was near dead, man. The police kicked me out of their car right there." He gestured to the main gates.

"The Pastor took me in, no questions asked. I could do nothing to start with. I was so ill from drugs I couldn't even wipe my butt!" He hooted with laughter at this, shaking his head at the thought of it. "I really was such a loser. But everyone here showed me love. And I'm back from the dead now. I was a bad, bad man before, but I just want to help others now. If it wasn't for The Pastor I'd be long gone."

"And I could have wound up dead." Uncle Antonio said quietly. "I was far from perfect too, Hal, just not careless enough to lose my hand like Jose here." He slapped his friend on the back. "All we ever need is someone on our side."

Hal nodded in agreement, amazed by these tales of love, drugs and incompetent bum wiping. When he looked up he spotted Gina, who had just walked back through the main gate laden with her shopping.

"Be with you in a few minutes," she shouted across at them. "Off to my room." Hal gave her a thumbs up.

The Pastor, Jose and Hal all fell quiet. The Pastor looked deep in thought, rubbing sand between his hands, and letting it trickle between his fingers.

"We are like a human junkyard here, Hal," he said, finally. "Full of lost souls that need recycling. Some make it and some don't, but it's important to love them no matter what."

The Pastor slowly stood up, groaning with the effort. "I've been lucky enough to be recycled and so has Jose here," he said, smirking. "And that really is a miracle considering he's only semi-house-trained!"

Jose hit The Pastor with his good arm and the old friends laughed as they play punched each other. Hal noticed Mexicans punched and grabbed and hugged each other a lot, very different to the handshakes of Craddly Hill.

After a while they all fell quiet again and watched as Rosalita finished shaving Jorge in his wheelchair. She washed his face clean with a flannel, kissed him on the forehead and gave his paralyzed body a long hug.

"Rosalita's still young, Hal," said The Pastor. "Just 16. Trust me, she's had a really hard time. She's angry and bitter. But look at her with Jorge." He pointed his stick towards them. "Just beautiful, hey. She'll be recycled one day too. Just you wait and see."

Wrong Time / Wrong Place / Wrong Girl

After dropping off her shopping in her room, Gina dashed back to join The Pastor, Jose and Hal in the courtyard. She'd bought herself a black shirt covered in gold stars. On her head was a wide-brimmed hat.

"Hey cowgirl," Hal said, whistling. "Looking good."

Gina flashed him a smile. "I can't believe this is only our second day here."

"Me too," Hal said. Craddly Hill, his mum, Abby and Mr B seemed like part of a distant world now. "It's been the most…"

Hal stopped mid-flow. "What's that noise?"

They all looked up at once. A black Jeep, revving its engines like a Formula One car, blazed through the main gates and scrunched to a halt in front of them in a cloud of dust. They stared at it in surprise, Gina's eyes on stalks.

"That's quite an entrance," said The Pastor. "It's probably the police with another lost soul to add to the family. Let's go and see, amigos." He gestured for Gina and Hal to join him.

"I don't like it, Pastor," whispered Jose, grabbing The Pastor's arm. "This isn't a normal police vehicle. And where are the security guys? Make sure to ask for ID."

"Oh, it's fine, Jose. You are getting jumpy in your old age. It might be the border patrol. They often drop off folks here too."

The Jeep's driver, a beefy guy with a red beret jumped out. He looked like a gorilla, crossed with a commando, but most worryingly, he was holding a rifle. He popped open the Jeep's trunk and dragged out a boy in his teens with long black hair and a leather jacket. The boy's hands, tied together with a rope, were stretched out in front of him.

The Pastor, all smiles, calmly introduced himself to the armed man with the red beret who babbled away in super quick Spanish.

"That boy in ropes has been threatening strangers in the town square in Ciudad Juárez," Gina said, translating for Hal. "He's been sedated and needs to go in one of the cells here. He's got a history of craziness."

Red Beret elbowed the roped-up boy in the stomach. The boy groaned and fell to his knees. His face was tense, his eyes darting all over the place. The Pastor raised his hand and helped lift the miserable looking prisoner up, smiled at him and asked him his name.

"Javier," the boy mumbled, brushing the dust off his jacket.

"So, we'll take Javier here to the cells," explained The Pastor. "It's for his own safety, just until he's calmed down. He might be a bit cranky for a while." He put his arm around Javier's shoulders.

"Jose," shouted The Pastor to his friend. "Open up the nearest cell please."

Jose was still eyeing up Red Beret suspiciously. He pulled out a string of keys with his good hand and pushed on the cell door. The hinge made a high-pitched screech as it opened.

By now, most of the other family members had started to crowd around, although Hal noticed there was no sign of Rosalita and Marco the Narco.

Red Beret was looking more and more jumpy and shouting things in Spanish so fast that even Gina was struggling to understand. He pushed the boy towards the open cell aggressively, holding his rifle up in the air like a cowboy.

"Mamma Mia," said Gina, shaking her head. "This is all pretty heavy. Something doesn't feel right."

Gina and Hal walked nearer to the cells to get a clearer view, Pancho padding along behind them.

A commotion kicked off up ahead. Hal could hear Jose shouting. It looked like he was arguing with Red Beret. No, worse. They were fighting! Jose was using his good arm in defense but it was doing little good. All of a sudden, Red Beret raised his rifle and brought it down hard. Jose staggered back holding his face and slumped against the cell walls.

While this was going on, somehow the prisoner, Javier, had managed to undo his rope and free his hands. He pulled out a pistol from his jacket and fired it repeatedly into the sand.

Fsht. Fsht. Fsht. Fsht.

The crack of the bullets echoed around the empty landscape.

Everyone stayed frozen to the spot except The Pastor who rushed over to check on Jose. He bent down over his old friend and cradled his bleeding head in his poncho.

Javier and Red Beret now waved their guns at the crowd in the courtyard. It was clear they were working together; the whole fake prisoner thing had just been a means to gain The Pastor's trust and get the cells open.

Hal looked at Gina. Her legs were shaking and her face was paralyzed with fear. Hal's heart was beating like crazy, blood throbbing round his head. This was all happening so suddenly. What was going on?

"*Manos arriba todo el mundo, ahora!*" shouted Red Beret. "Hands up everyone. Right away!"

"This is bad," whispered Gina, her voice shrill. "I can't even text for help now."

They all put their hands up, except the family members who were too mentally unwell to understand. One of them was even laughing. Lupita, Hal thought. *Please be quiet, Loopy Lou*, he said softly to himself, *these guys mean business.*

Red Beret shouted something to Javier.

"What did he say?" Hal whispered to Gina.

"Not sure. It sounded like: 'find the girl.'"

Hal could see The Pastor pleading with Red Beret to explain what was going on. Red Beret was listening, calm and patient. But the pistol-waving boy, Javier, wasn't having any of it. He moved forward and hit the Pastor in the face. Javier had chunky rings on his fingers, Hal noticed, so it must have hurt. The Pastor's nose was now bleeding.

After the punches, Javier screamed a stream of insults; he had a lot of violence in him for someone so young. The Pastor smiled sadly at him and, using his poncho, wiped the blood from his face. He then turned his attention back to the wounded Jose.

Behind Hal and Gina, Lupita begin to wail. The rest of the family was quiet now, united in terror. Their whole world, with The Pastor and Jose usually at the center of it, was in ruins.

And it was about to get worse.

Javier barked some orders in Spanish. The Pastor helped up Jose, who was still very unsteady on his legs, and ushered him into the cell –all the time with crazy boy Javier waving a gun at them. Once this was done, Red Beret locked the door on the pair of them.

Javier raised his pistol and scanned the crowd in front of him. His gaze stopped at Gina. He moved stealthily forward, pointing his gun in front of him as if in a cop film.

"Could he really be heading for Gina?" thought Hal. Clearly he was. Within thirty seconds he was standing directly in front of her. The sun was beating down and Hal was sweating enough to fill up the Rio Grande. It was all like a terrible dream.

Javier shouted some commands. He looked so young, no more than 18, but his face was hard and his eyes mean. They looked like eyes that would happily kill someone.

"He's telling us to move to the Jeep," said Gina. She was near tears.

"It's ok," Hal told her, grabbing her hand, but his voice was shaking too.

"I wish my dad was here," she whispered.

"Me too," Hal said.

Gina's dad was back in England and Hal's dad had driven to Ciudad Juárez earlier that morning to buy some equipment for his documentary and drink 'a cup of decent coffee'. *Great timing, Dad!,* thought Hal.

When they reached the Jeep, Javier told Gina to sit in the back seat. She was shaking so much now; it was like she had malaria. "Don't panic, Gina," Hal reassured her, strengthening his hold on her hand, but she was in a state of shock, not really aware of what was going on.

"You!" snapped Javier to Hal, "step back!"

Before Gina or Hal could move there was another shout across the courtyard. It was Marco the Narco. He was holding Rosalita at gunpoint, pushing what looked like a pistol towards her forehead. Behind the main gate Hal noticed The Pastor's two security guards had been gagged and tied up. Just great! What was going on? Hal thought. Marco was supposed to be Rosalita's guardian, not pointing guns at her.

"What's Marco saying, Gina?" Hal asked.

"That I've kidnapped the wrong, girl," interrupted Javier coolly. He spoke perfect English. "Marco says he has the right one over there with him." Javier smiled grimly and gestured towards Rosalita. "I think he's a bit angry with me."

Why would anyone want to kidnap Rosalita? Hal thought. *This is all too weird.*

"But this Gina is such a beauty," said Javier. He stretched his neck over Gina's shoulder. "I think I might keep her anyway." He ran his fingers through her hair. Gina started to freak out, shouting at Javier.

"Shut up, my beauty," he said in his oily voice. But Gina wouldn't, she had become hysterical. She was crying uncontrollably and lashed out. Javier didn't even flinch, just quickly put his pistol against her head. "Calm down, my beauty," he said. His pistol was at her temple. "I like you, but trust me, I will shoot if I have to."

Hal looked on appalled. Gina was now breathing like she was suffocating, lots of short, tight breaths. She was badly panicked, in the sort of state where she might do anything.

"Calm down," Javier repeated, struggling to control her.

"Leave her!" barked Marco the Narco, appearing with Rosalita.

Marco may have been oldish with a wart on his nose but he had real authority today, thought Hal. He looked as hard as nails. Marco took the pistol away from Rosalita's forehead, but kept a firm grip on her arm. "This is the girl you want," he told Javier.

The gagged Rosalita was struggling frantically. But with her hands and mouth tied there was little she could do. Marco shoved her into the back of the truck and began to tie her legs too.

"Come on, Señor Marco, let's take this beauty," said Javier, tightening his grip on Gina.

"No," said Marco firmly. Hal sensed he was the leader of them. "Leave her."

"What a waste," said Javier, lowering his gun and touching Gina's cheek. "Such a pretty little hummingbird, aren't you?"

At this moment something in Gina must have snapped. She shrieked like a wild animal and dug her nails hard into Javier's face, biting into the hand that was touching her. Javier screamed in pain as he wrestled her off.

"You little witch," he shouted, pulling on Gina's hair. "How dare you bite me! What are you, a dog?" As they struggled Gina's head bashed against the Jeep bonnet. There was a dull thud and she slumped to the ground, sprawled out on the sand. Her new shirt was ripped and her hat crumpled. At least Hal could see she was still breathing.

Hal was instantly filled with rage, ready for blood. Although the signs had been pretty obvious over the last few days, it was at that exact moment he realized he would do anything, anything at all, for Gina Moreno. Eat *menudo*, slay dragons, destroy anyone who tried to hurt her…

Without thinking, Hal smashed his fist into Javier's face. After this he kneed him low in his belly. Javier dropped his pistol and fell backwards, landing hard on the sand. After a few seconds he lunged for his gun but Marco already had his foot on it.

"I have to shoot him," gasped Javier, stabbing his finger at Hal, his eyes watery with pain. "He cannot do that. Kick me here," he clutched between his legs, "and live."

"We don't want anyone getting killed," snapped Marco. "We can take him with us and deal with him later." Javier nodded reluctantly in agreement.

Marco looked at Hal and shrugged. "Sorry, Ginger." He raised a fist. Hal felt an explosion of pain above his nose and his legs gave way. He fell flat on the ground, blinking sand from his eyes. Gina was lying next to him, still looking a bit groggy. Hal focused his gaze on her.

"I'm sorry I couldn't protect you," Hal whispered, slurring his words a bit. Gina smiled and reached out her hand. She was too weak to reach him, but her eyes looked strong.

"Take the boy and leave the girl," ordered Marco to Javier. "And make it quick."

Javier, still sore from his wounds, pulled Gina away from the Jeep and left her lying under a mesquite. Sorry, you were hurt, Gina Moreno, Hal thought, but you'll be safe now.

A couple of the young Mexican volunteers rushed over to tend Gina, followed by a tearful Lupita. Red Beret appeared. He crouched down and lifted Hal up as if he was a dead man. Hal had no strength left at all and his head felt like it wasn't really his. Marco clearly had a mean right hook. Hal wasn't so much seeing stars as the whole flipping solar system. He also badly wanted to be sick.

Red Beret dumped Hal next to Rosalita in the back of the Jeep. Even though she was gagged and tied up, you only needed to see her eyes to realize she was ready to take on anyone. Hal almost felt sorry for the kidnappers. For some reason, despite the grim situation and a brain-busting headache, he found this pretty funny.

The last thing he remembered was Pancho jumping into the Jeep and licking his face. Then darkness.

The Cave

When Hal woke his head felt sore but not nearly as bad as before. He shuffled up in his seat. His hands had been tied but at least his mouth hadn't been gagged.

Rosalita was still beside him, gagged and tied, eyes like lasers of hate. Part of Hal was happy she couldn't speak. He dreaded to think what toxic insults she'd come up with once freed.

Pancho was sitting between them, panting heavily. Seeing Hal sit up he licked his face. Hal moved his bound hands and stroked the loyal dog as best he could. He smiled at Rosalita to try and reassure her. Hal couldn't tell if she smiled back, but from the look in her eyes, he didn't think so.

In the front of the Jeep, Red Beret was driving. Marco the Narco was leaning out of the passenger window while Javier sat between them by the gear lever. Javier looked even more like a baby-faced kid next to two such hulks. They were travelling very fast through the desert. Hal glanced at his watch. It was only midday - he couldn't have been out of it for long.

"Can I have some water?" Hal asked. His mouth was as dry as the desert that surrounded them.

Marco and Javier both turned back to look at him.

"Woken up have you, little worm?" said Javier, jutting out his jaw. "Worms don't need water." Javier's face was badly scratched from his fight with Gina and his left hand was wrapped in a bandage from her bites. *Nice work, Gina Moreno*, thought Hal.

Marco was a bit more sympathetic.

"Here," he said, handing over a plastic bottle to Hal, "but none for that monkey next to you. She nearly bit my fingers off tying her up." Hal shrugged at Rosalita, as if to say: 'sorry', and took a few glugs of the warm water.

In the rear view mirror Hal could see some movement. What was it? No, it couldn't be. Yes, it was! His dad and the The Pastor in the beat up red truck. Hal squinted – it was a long way off but, yes, his dad was coming to the rescue.

"Don't worry, little worm, they won't catch us," sneered Javier, seeing where Hal was looking. "They've been following for a while." He flicked his fingers. "But we can outrace them just like that and…" He gestured to the floor in front of him, where various guns were stashed, "remember, we have all these lovely toys too."

"Oh, no, stay away, Dad!" Hal thought. *"These guys will shoot you without batting an eyelid."* But part of him was also happy his dad and The Pastor knew where he was, it also meant Gina and Jose would all be getting help. And surely the police would be on to these three vicious jokers soon.

"I think we should shake them up a bit, Ginger, don't you?" said Marco the Narco.

He picked up a gun under his seat. It looked like some sort of machine gun. He cocked it and opened the passenger window fully. As he was leaning out, preparing to aim, a distant siren sounded off.

"Ah ha, here come the cops, poor fools," said Marco, calm as always. "Let's pull over."

Did I hear right, thought Hal. He couldn't believe it. Why would Marco want to pull over now? Did he want to turn himself in? Was it a trap?

Red Beret braked and they screeched to a halt, skidding across the tarmac and onto the edge of the sand. Marco jumped out. Hal heard him rummaging in the Jeep's boot.

Wrenching his head round Hal could see the police car had already caught up with his dad and The Pastor. The two vehicles had slowed down. The Pastor was now talking to the police through his window, Hal could just about make out his purple poncho in the distance.

After a short conversation, The Pastor pulled over and only the police car remained in pursuit. The Pastor must have been told to stay away. "*Good*", Hal thought, "*Dad is safe*".

Hal twisted his head further round. It was hard to see what was going on in the boot but Marco was making lots of loud, clanking noises. Then Hal caught a glimpse of what he was holding. Oh no! No, no, no! A rocket launcher!

Hal's head was pulsing. That thing could blow the police car to smithereens. He had to do something. Rosalita was also straining to look what was going on, but between the two of them, they were as good as useless. Hal thought of pretending to have a fit, or to start screaming or...but it was too late. Marco was already standing up and taking aim.

Seconds later a hissing noise was followed by a humungous blast. Beside Hal, Pancho nearly leapt out his skin. He barked a couple of times and then sat shivering, drooling onto Hal's lap.

In the wing mirror all Hal could see at first was smoke. Then he turned his head and saw the full damage. The missile had at least missed the police car but hit the tarmac in front. The vehicle had zoomed off the road, skidding wildly and landed on its side. It looked like the driver and his partner would be ok, but no way were the police going to catch up with them anytime soon.

Marco jumped back in the passenger seat, grinning. Javier held up his gun and said some words in Spanish. It was clear he wanted to finish the policemen off. Marco growled and took the weapon from his hands.

"*Vámonos!*" he ordered. "Let's go. Why do you want to kill everyone, Javier!" Red Beret floored it, and off they sped again.

"They will send helicopters next," Hal shouted, angry about the police car, angry that he was completely powerless, angry that he was tied up next to Rosalita Sourface and not hanging out with beautiful Gina Moreno.

"My dad will find you, I know he will," Hal warned, but he wasn't sure he sounded very convincing.

Javier started to laugh, a cruel, joyless noise, not really a laugh at all.

"Stupid worm thinks Daddy will save him," he said, swiveling his head back to look at Hal, "we are going where nobody will find you, you fool."

Hal was on the verge of tears but reined them in. He didn't want to give Javier the satisfaction of seeing him crack.

"But you are right, Hal," said Marco, almost kindly. "They will send helicopters. And thanks to your dad and The Pastor the police got to us much faster than I thought." He shrugged his massive shoulders, "but you see, I'm afraid it's too late. We're already here."

Red Beret braked and swerved the Jeep off down a dirt track. In the distance Hal could see a white building shimmering in the heat. It looked like a run-down villa; there were big gaps in the roof where the tiles had caved in. As they approached a group of men in overalls opened a metal gate to the side of the building.

Marco pulled a remote control device from his pocket and prodded it. A massive hole, about the size of a swimming pool, slowly opened up ahead of them. Red Beret looked like he was going to crash straight into it, but at the last minute slowed right down and inched very slowly to the edge. The Jeep jolted forward onto a steep concrete ramp.

As they drove down into the darkness Red Beret flipped the Jeep's headlights on and revealed an underground world: a gigantic garage. It was big and grey and almost empty except for a few wooden chairs, a fridge, some scrunched up drink cans and pile of old newspapers. A fake skeleton with a hat leant against the fridge, smiling at them. The floor was horribly stained with something. Hal didn't want to know what.

It was the creepiest place Hal had ever seen. Pancho whimpered beside him while Rosalita continued to make muffled groans through her gag.

"Welcome to *La Cueva*," said Javier, narrowing his eyes at Hal. "That means The Cave, you little worm." He smiled. "No-one will ever find you here. Or Monkey girl. It's the end of the road for the pair of you."

Señor Slimy

When Marco ripped off Rosalita's gag and finally gave her some water she didn't say a word. Not a squeak. Sure, she spat water in Marco's face and glared at him like he was the foulest man that ever walked the earth, but not one curse came out of her normally vicious mouth.

Then she turned to Hal. He smiled, hoping they were friends, on the same team now. Clearly not: Rosalita looked at him like he was the second foulest man on earth.

"You threw up on my lap in the Jeep!" Rosalita hissed at Hal, after their kidnappers left them to talk above ground. "You are a *cabroncito!*"

"Sorry, Marco the Narco's punch must have made me sick," Hal said. "To be fair I was pretty out of it." After a pause he asked: "So what's *cabroncito* mean? Does it mean I'm cool? A genius?"

"Billy goat,' she said coldly. "It means you're a little Billy goat, but much worse".

"That's charming. Thanks."

Wow, Rosalita, Hal thought: *"Of all the creepy underground caves, in all the deserts, in all the world, you have to choose this one."* Hal wished he could have shared this with his dad –it was a bit like a line from Johnny Bradby's favorite movie: *Casablanca*, which was about 1,000 years old and shot in black and white. As a joke, Hal's dad said the line to his mum sometimes: *"Of all the houses, in all the streets, in all the world, you have to choose 21, Pond Place, Craddly Hill"*. Hal certainly wasn't going to share the joke with Rosalita. She'd already spat at him enough.

"You really are a ginger-haired freak, aren't you?" Rosalita added, clearly thinking she hadn't been mean enough to Hal already.

If we are talking freaks, Rosi, Hal thought, just take a good look in the mirror, but decided to stay quiet.

"Is ginger freak worse than *cabroncito*?" Hal replied. "Or a little better? Perhaps you are starting to like me." Rosalita turned towards Hal and spat again.

"Please! Can you just stop spitting?" Hal sighed, wiping his face with his bound hands. "Not just at me. Stop spitting at everyone. At Gina, at Marco, at the whole world!" Hal looked straight at her. "Just *what* is your problem?" Rosalita spat again, hitting Hal square in the face.

Pancho started whimpering. Hal shunted himself across the seat and plunged his face into the nervous dog's coat. Hal couldn't believe what was happening. A few hours ago he had been laughing with Gina. He was the happiest he'd ever been in his life. And now he was stuck in an underground hovel with a bunch of violent thugs and a mouthy sidekick with ice flowing through her veins. Even the smiling skeleton hanging on the wall seemed like better company.

Thank goodness for Pancho, my only friend down here, Hal thought. He breathed in his dog's coat and stroked his ears. "It's ok, boy," Hal said, sinking his face further into Pancho's coat, as if to block out the awful fix he was in. He was holding back tears: "We'll be just fine."

"Oh, no *cabroncito*, come on!" said Rosalita, with a cruel little laugh. "You aren't crying are you? Crying like a little girl. That's all we need."

"Just shut up, Rosalita," Hal shouted, lifting his head up sharply. "Shut up, ok!" He felt Pancho flinching beneath him as his voice got louder. At least he'd got Rosalita's attention.

"Yes, I'm crying," he said, more calmly now. "I tried not to, but I'm 14-years-old and you are my only friend here, and you are treating me like scum." He wiped at his tears with his roped hands. "One weeks ago I'd never once left England. I'd never left my parents and my little sister and my dog." He wiped his face again. "And now I am here in Mexico, kidnapped, stuck in the cave from hell. Nobody knows where I am. I might never be seen again and all you can do is spit at me and shout at me and insult me and…"

"Well, at least I didn't throw up on you," snapped Rosalita. "Just grow up, *cabroncito*."

That was it! Rosalita was officially made of ice, The Wicked Witch of Juárez. He hated her.

"Gina was right," Hal said, trying to keep his cool. "You really are a cow. A monkey-faced cow!" He strained desperately against his ropes. "Who in their right mind would kidnap you? And why Marco? At least tell me why. Is it for your beautiful face? Your lovely sense of humor, your sweet…"

"That's more like it, *cabroncito*!" Rosalita sneered. "Come on. Hit me with it. I knew you had fire in your belly somewhere." She paused, chin jutting Hal's way. "So what do you want to say next, hey? Come on I've heard them all. How about scar-faced pig?" She spat out the words, poison in her eyes. "Skew-eyed monster? Squashed-nosed dog? Ugly…."

"Shut up!" Hal shouted. "Just shut up…"

"Nice to hear you kids getting on so well." Marco appeared at the top of the trap door, with Javier in tow. "You really make a lovely pair."

They walked towards Hal and Rosalita, their footsteps echoing around the dingy garage. Marco opened the back door of the Jeep and dragged Rosalita out by her arm. She kicked out at him, but with both her legs tied made little impact.

"You dirty Judas, Marco." Rosalita spoke softly, but with great passion. "You pretend to be a man of honor, but you are just a traitor." She looked him hard in the eyes as she struggled. "My father will track you down and kill you, you know that don't you? He'll kill you all."

"You are probably right, *guapa*," replied Marco, holding her firmly. Hal knew *guapa* meant beautiful, he was being sarcastic. "But you should know we have asked your daddy for ransom money. Only one million pesos – a very affordable sum for his darling Rosalita." Marco shrugged. "And you know what? He isn't willing to give a bean. Not a single *frijol*!"

"I wouldn't either," said Javier, laughing. "If I had a monkey for a daughter."

"You are liars." Rosalita looked furious and upset all at once. "Tomas Ceto always looks after family. He will find me, even in this place. You wait."

It sounded a bit more convincing than telling them his dad would find them, Hal thought, *but not much.* As hopeless situations go this was up there with the best of them. Rosalita and him weren't so much the underdogs, they were the underground dogs, without a soul to hear their howling. It was like Marco and Javier were football giants Manchester United and Rosalita and him were plucky pygmies, Sheffield Wednesday.

But something was bugging him. What did Rosalita say?

"Tomas Ceto always looks after family."

That name was so familiar but his thoughts were dazed, all over the place. Then he remembered in a flash, all those newspaper reports:

WHERE IS THE TOAD?

Hal pictured the big man with the big moustache looking like big trouble.

Oh great, just great. As if things couldn't get any worse Hal realized his fate now lay in the hands of Mexico's most vicious criminal and how much he was willing to pay for Rosalita, his psycho daughter. Now it was all clear – the butterfly tattoo and necklace. Of course, realized Hal. Rosalita was Mariposa, The Little Butterfly he'd seen on the news. But he thought she was probably dead. And how could that sweet child with marigolds in her hair turn into the spit-happy fruitcake sitting next to him.

If it was true that Tomas Ceto had decided not to pay a bean for Rosalita – and

Hal had to say, he didn't blame him – then what? Would his dad pay instead?

Hal smiled at the idea of Johnny Bradby having to fork out. For a man who wore second-hand clothes, cut his own hair, cycled everywhere to save a few gallons of gas and had the oldest brick of a cellphone ever, then ten million pesos sounded quite a bit to fork out. But Hal also knew his mum and dad would do anything to save him if they had to.

Hal leaned his face into Pancho again. The poor dog looked spooked from all that was going on.

"Sorry boy," he whispered, "but at least we've got each other."

Then he felt Marco's arm on his collar yanking him up out of the Jeep.

*

Marco shoved Rosalita and Hal onto a couple of wooden chairs, their legs and hands still tied. Pancho laid down at Hal's feet on the hard concrete floor. The skeleton with the hat stared at them from against the fridge.

The trapdoor above them buzzed open again, letting in a ray of sunlight. A well-dressed man in a black leather jacket with puffed up, heavily gelled hair walked down the ramp. He looked like he was about to sing on X Factor.

"Papi!" shouted Javier, and rushed up to hug the new man. Papi! For Hal the word hit home how young Javier was.

Papi gave Javier two kisses on his cheeks, then looked up at Hal and Rosalita, his smile beaming, teeth like snow. He looked very different to the thuggish Marco and commando-like Red Beret.

"And who do we have here?" Papi gave another big smile. "Is it young Hal?"

"Hal hit and kicked me, Papi," Javier blurted out. "I want to hurt him…"

"Gina was the one who hurt you," Hal interrupted. "A 14-year-old girl in a frilly shirt. You must be so proud."

"Stop lying, ginger worm." Javier walked up and slapped him hard in the face. After Marco's earlier punch Hal hardly felt it.

"Calm down, Javier. All in good time." Papi spoke slowly with a deep, smooth voice. It was a comforting voice, but Hal didn't trust it. This was Javier's father after all - and look how Javier had turned out.

Papi walked over to Rosalita.

"We met once, my dear," he said, standing in front of her. "Years ago. I don't expect you remember. You were still very beautiful then." He laughed and swept a hand through his long hair as Rosalita gave him a vicious stare. It was clear Javier's father was even slimier than his son.

"Your father and I go back a long way you see, Rosi," said Señor Slimy. "I'm sorry your dad is being so mean with your ransom money. It's not like he can't afford it."

He leaned directly in front of Rosalita and grabbed hold of her left ear. "Maybe we could send him one of your pretty little ears." He twisted Rosalita's ear as he spoke. "That might make daddy open up his safe. Sadly, your face has seen better days already, hey, my little angel?"

Hal noticed that to her credit Rosalita didn't rise to the bait, just sat, staring hard at the floor, until Slimy released his grip.

"This is our secret cave," added Slimy, gesturing around the gloomy garage. "Hardly anyone knows about it. We enjoy having dog fights here, as you can see from the blood on the floor."

So that's what those stains were, thought Hal. Gross! No wonder Pancho seemed so tense.

"But don't worry, Hal," said Señor Slimy. "You can keep your dog for now."

He gave another one of his 100-tooth, X Factor smiles. *And tonight Simon I will be a cruel, greasy drug lord with Cheryl Cole hair and epic burger breath.*

"What will happen to Pancho after we go?" Hal asked.

"Oh, we'll train him up for dog fights." Señor Slimy winked at Hal. "He's a good strong dog, just a bit soft at the moment. We'll soon work that out of him."

"You didn't think we'd keep him for a pet, did you, worm boy?" butted in Javier. "Aww, sweet little puppy Pancho."

"Moron," Hal said under his breath.

"You'll be happy to hear we are having a dog fight tonight, Hal," added Señor Slimy, ignoring Hal's insult to his son. "You and Rosalita can have front row seats. It's two pit bull terriers. Both very fierce. Grrr." Señor Slimy growled and pawed his hand towards Rosalita. "Pancho can see what he is letting himself in for."

Hal suddenly felt very tired and sad. He'd had enough of insults and threats. It was so different from all the fun of *Miracles in Hell*: Dad, Gina, The Pastor, Jose and the gang. *That's my world with them*, thought Hal, *not this horrible dark place.*

Hal pictured his mum and Abby and Mr B and wondered if news had reached them in Craddly Hill yet. His mum would be all over the place. She'd been bad enough with Pancho getting lost, let alone her only son. Hal's eyes welled up but he managed to stop full on blubbing.

Over the last hours Hal, Rosalita and Pancho had only drunk a few gulps of water. Hal wanted to stay upbeat but he was feeling really weak and ground down now.

"Is there any way out of this?" thought Hal, for the hundredth time.

Rosalita was certainly offering no support – the opposite in fact, and they were both in the hands of a brutal father son combination, in a place no one would find them. They didn't really stand much of a chance.

"The dog fight starts at seven o'clock sharp," said Señor Slimy, walking towards the trap door entrance. "Don't forget will you. No need for tickets." He turned and beamed at Hal. "My treat."

Marco the Narco

Once the trapdoor had slammed shut, it was just Rosalita and Hal again.

"So you are Tomas Ceto's daughter," Hal said, trying to sound casual. "That's why you...sorry, *we*, have been kidnapped."

Silence.

"Rosalita, I really think we need to start talking. If we have any chance at all, we need to work together."

Rosalita continued staring at the floor. She kicked out her legs in frustration.

Silence.

"Great," Hal said. "So unless you are being rude to everyone, you don't speak at all." He paused. "I hate to say this, but it's clearly all down to you that I'm here. Trust me, no one would want to kidnap me, a school kid from Craddly Hill, unless they wanted my soccer kit and Harry Potter books." He sighed, then silence. "Ok then, let's just sit here sulking. That will really help."

Silence.

Several minutes ticked by. Rosalita continued staring at her feet. Hal thought he'd try a different approach.

"For what it's worth, Rosalita," he said. "I thought you did really well not to let Javier's dad get to you. Wow, he's such a jerk. What's his story?"

Rosalita looked up and turned towards Hal. She looked at him for a long time and finally gave him a hint of a smile. It really was the smallest of smiles but after all her meanness it felt like sun breaking through the clouds.

"Javier's dad's called *Chico Guapo* – Pretty Boy," said Rosalita, her voice calm and soft. "He's my father's biggest rival. They are the two big gangsters fighting for control of Juárez."

Rosalita is talking to me, Hal thought, *hallelujah!* A spark of hope swelled inside him.

"My dad's known for being brutal," Rosalita continued. "But Pretty Boy Sánchez is even worse. He will kill anyone. Dad will only hurt other people involved in crime, Pretty Boy will hurt women, kids, he doesn't care."

"Wow," Hal said. "He sounds like a monster."

"He's called Pretty Boy because he's so vain," said Rosalita. "He's spent loads on plastic surgery to keep his looks."

"It didn't work. He looks like Dracula with hair gel."

Rosalita smiled again, a bit bigger this time.

"You're ok, *cabroncito*," she said, looking across at Hal. "I'm sorry I was so mean to you." She let out a long sigh. "I'm just so *angry* with everything. Marco was the person I trusted most in the world and now even he has betrayed me. Totally sold me out."

"Yeah, you two seemed very close at The Pastor's," Hal said. "I'm really sorry." He paused. "And I'm sorry about all that stuff I called you."

"What, you mean, monkey-faced cow," she grinned. "That was pretty good, *cabroncito*. But to be fair, I called you a ginger haired freak."

"Yes you did! And you spat at me about 10 times." They both laughed awkwardly and then fell silent, the only noise the whirring of the fridge.

"Do you really think your dad won't pay out any money for you?" Hal asked. Rosalita stayed quiet and Hal was worried he had upset her.

"I hate my father," she said, her voice fierce. "Really hate him. I used to love him. I have an elder sister, Sol, and when we were growing up I was always his favorite." She smiled sadly. "But after my surgery and once I understood what his job was, that he was a gangster, that he hurt people, I challenged him. He didn't like that." She paused, a far away look in her eyes. "One time I saw him shouting at my mom and I charged at him. He slapped me in the face. After that, I lost all love for him." Her eyes narrowed. "Sol is now his darling, like she always wanted."

"I'm sorry, that really sucks," Hal said, happy that Rosalita was now sharing this with him. "But even so, he is your father. He should pay up as a matter of honor."

"Oh, don't worry," replied Rosalita. "He will make all the right noises. Say in public that he will do anything to save his darling daughter, but trust me, he won't give a *peso*." She spat on the floor. "He hates me, hates the fact I don't obey him. I left the family to volunteer for The Pastor as a way to escape that life. Dad sent Marco to keep an eye on me."

"I'd heard that Marco was your uncle." Hal paused. "That he'd stood by you when you went off the rails."

Rosalita laughed and shook her head. She explained to Hal that was just a made up story, so no one would suspect her of being Tomas Ceto's daughter. Marco played the role of her uncle, so no one would suspect him either: even his wart was fake. The Pastor was known for taking in anyone, no questions asked: he had no idea who they both really were.

"So Marco worked for your dad for ages?" Hal was getting confused. "Then why is he helping Pretty Boy Sánchez now?"

"Pretty Boy must have paid him more," Rosalita rolled her eyes. "Made a deal with him, so he'd help kidnap me. Marco will end up dead sooner or later. Even narcos can only betray each other so many times."

They fell quiet again. Hal was glad to learn all these facts but it didn't improve his chances of escape much. He decided not to say he already knew she was the Little Butterfly: that could wait. Had Pretty Boy something to do with those wounds of hers? And what about Sol, her elder sister, Tomas Ceto's heir in the making? Where was she now?

"So how are we going to get out of here?" Hal asked. "Do you think we can start bargaining with Pretty Boy?"

"Well, *cabroncito*, I've got about three pesos in my pockets," said Rosalita, smiling. "They want one million for me but I expect three pesos is about all you're worth. I'll have you out of here in no time."

*

After this, things were pretty cool between Rosalita and Hal. It was like a dark cloud had lifted. Well, not so much a cloud, but a full on tropical storm, judging from how moody and mouthy she'd been before. Hal understood why now though. Being the daughter of one of Mexico's most dangerous criminals must have been the worst childhood ever.

Rosalita still called Hal *cabroncito* and occasionally spat on the floor if he mentioned someone she didn't like – especially Pretty Boy Sánchez or her father – but they were definitely more of a team now.

They even pinged around a few ideas for escaping. Sadly, all of them involved them having their arms and legs untied. This seemed unlikely as the only time this happened was for the bathroom, and even then they were guarded at gunpoint.

Their only hope was from the outside, but their cell phones had been taken, Tomas Ceto wasn't paying up and nobody else had a clue where they were. Hal realized their options were running out fast.

The trapdoor swung open providing a brief glimpse of the starry evening sky. Pretty Boy and Javier strutted down the garage's ramp, both in their black leather jackets. Behind them was Marco with two pit bull terriers. The dogs, one black, one white, were straining at their leads. Both had muzzles strapped tight around their snouts. Beneath Hal's feet, Pancho sat bolt upright, looking very tense.

"Don't worry, Pancho," said Javier, giving the frightened dog a stroke. "You'll get your chance to fight once we've toughened you up." He smiled. "Oh, and said goodbye to your owner." Hal's gut churned in fear but he tried not to show it.

"These pit bulls will fight each other to the death," added Javier, gesturing to the fierce little dogs. "The survivor will be rested, fed up and next month go and fight in a warehouse near Mexico City." He grinned. "It's a great event – a bit like the dog fighting Olympics."

"Doesn't a young guy like you have any better hobbies than dog fighting, Javier?" said Rosalita. "How about salsa dancing. Or knitting?"

"Shut up, monkey girl." He shot her an angry look. "You're in no position to talk. Your dad still won't give us any money."

"That doesn't surprise me anymore." She frowned. "And by the way it won't make any difference if you send him my ear. He hates me. You picked the wrong girl."

"Oh dear," said Pretty Boy. "We'll have to think of something else then because the alternative is…"He paused and looked at the luminous skeleton on the wall. "Well, I think you know what the alternative is, my dear?"

"Oh yes, I know," said Rosalita, calmly.

Pretty Boy pointed at the skeleton.

"We have this skeleton here, Hal," he said, gesturing like a teacher. "To remind us that life is short. Here in Mexico we have a charming festival called the Day of the Dead. It's next month you know. It's a time when we get together to celebrate the lives of our departed ancestors." He smiled. "You in

England are all a bit, how should I say, uptight about death, aren't you, Hal. But in Mexico we are more relaxed, talk about it, celebrate it, remember our loved ones."

He grinned at Rosalita. His teeth were so unnaturally bright Hal imagined them glowing in the dark like the skeleton. "We don't want the Day of the Dead to be real in your case, do we Rosi darling?"

"Tell me, Pretty Boy," said Rosalita. "Are you already dead? It's just that you look very like Dracula."

The gangster's smile slipped for a second, then returned.

"Very amusing." He paused, and fondled his hair. "By the way, Rosi dear, we thought we would place bets on the dogs tonight." He sneered at her. "If the white one wins, I shoot Hal. If the black one wins, I don't. He's of no use to us really is he? What do you think, young Hal?"

"I've got a better idea," Hal said.

"Do tell us, dear boy," gushed Pretty Boy.

"If the white one wins, Javier gets shot. And if the black one wins, oh, let's keep it simple, Javier gets shot too."

Javier ripped out a pistol from his leather jacket and pointed it at Hal.

"I'm gonna shoot him Papi, right now." Javier looked completely crazy, his teeth clenched, the whites of his eyes flashing. Hal flinched as he felt his gun hard on his temple. He closed his eyes, preparing for the worst.

A loud thump.

Hal felt the pressure of the gun ease and opened his eyes. Javier was slumped at his feet, groaning. Marco was standing above him, pointing his gun at Pretty Boy.

"What are you doing Marco, my friend?" Pretty Boy was visibly shaken but still just about keeping his cool. "Put the gun down and let's talk about this in a civilized way."

"A civilized way," said Marco. "That would be a first, Pretty Boy."

"Ok, well if you want to talk money, that's fine. A bigger cut perhaps?"

"For once this is not about money." Marco snapped. "For the first time in my life it's about doing the right thing. This girl here.' He pointed at Rosalita. "Is the bravest person I know. She stood up to her father the moment she realized he was a monster. She tried to protect her mother who was too weak to stand up for herself. She's the best person I've ever met. And all the time I sat back and never helped her."

"How touching," said Slimy. "But surely…"

"Shut up, you monster!" shouted Marco. "I'm not finished. And I want you to listen."

"I'm all ears," said Pretty Boy, sounding a bit tense now.

"As you know, five years ago Tomas Ceto's car was attacked," continued Marco. "A biker drove up to the passenger window and blasted it with a shotgun." He shook his head at the memory. "Rosalita, or Mariposa then, was the passenger. Aged 11. The blast peppered her beautiful face. She was the only one hurt. Tomas Ceto, Sol and me." His nose twitched in anger. "Were shaken but unharmed."

Marco walked over to Pretty Boy, pointing the gun at his head.

"I always remembered the face of the biker." He paused and looked hard at Pretty Boy. "It was you, wasn't it, you sick madman? Rather than shoot Tomas Ceto or me you go for an 11-year-old girl." Marco spat at the floor. "And Javier takes after you. He'd have killed Hal at The Pastor's. I only kidnapped him to calm your crazy boy down."

"We are gangsters, Marco," said Pretty Boy, sounding much more nervous now. "Power. Revenge. This is what we do."

"Shoot 11-year-old girls!" shouted Marco. "Threaten 14-year-old boys! This is not what we do. It's what *you* do."

"Why didn't you tell me, Marco," said Rosalita softly. There were tears rolling down her cheeks. "I thought you had betrayed me. It broke my heart."

"I would *never* betray you, Mariposa," said Marco tenderly, but keeping his gun firmly on Pretty Boy. "It's a long time since I've been able to call you that name. It feels good." He smiled at her. "But I needed to completely gain this fool's trust. If I'd told you about the kidnap plan, we would have been caught. I had to keep it real in order to get to him." He winked at her. "Now we can get our revenge."

"Marco!" Hal shouted.

From the floor, the wounded Javier had pulled out his gun. A shot rang out and Marco fell backwards.

From his chair Hal kicked out with his tied feet, winding Javier. Pretty Boy was also grabbing for a gun. Marco clutched his neck, where the bullet had skimmed, but managed to regain his balance. He fired twice at Pretty Boy, one shot hitting him in the leg. Pretty Boy shrieked and fell to the floor.

Javier was recovering. Hal kicked at him again and Rosalita, who had shuffled over, collapsed on top of him in her chair. The gun skidded out of his hand as Rosalita made contact. Javier screamed in pain, then snivelled quietly.

The two Pit Bulls had both been tearing around, but after the gunshots lay spooked and panting under a chair.

Marco quickly untied Rosalita and Hal. Rosalita had a big, purple bruise forming on her forehead where she had landed on Javier. But it can't have been hurting too much - she had the biggest smile on her face Hal had ever seen. Marco's wound looked like nothing more than a nick on his neck.

"I want you two to wait by the trap door," said Marco. "I have a bit of surgery I want to perform on Pretty Boy. Just need to use my knife."

He pulled out a huge blade from a sheath in his Jeans. It was more like a machete.

"Don't worry, I won't hurt him much." Marco felt the blade with his finger.

"But the one thing Pretty Boy can't stand is scars. Anyone messing with his pretty face." He looked at Rosalita. "I just need a tiny bit of payback."

Rosalita and Hal both shuffled over to the trap door entrance with Pancho. Hal wanted to take the pit bulls too but Rosi said they would be impossible to tame now they were fighting dogs. She found the remote control for the trap door and pointed it up.

"We should wait for Marco," she said, hesitating with the button. "There will be guards."

After a muffled scream from Pretty Boy, Marco reappeared.

Rosi pressed the remote button and the trapdoor slowly opened and the three of them jumped out into the cool evening air.

"Don't worry about the security guards," said Marco, quickening his pace. "I put some sleeping powder in their drinks earlier." As they ran Hal caught a glimpse of Red Beret out cold on a chair, a machine gun lying at his feet like a strange pet.

"Quick, follow me," shouted Marco. "*Vamos*. Let's go! Run, run!"

They all sprinted across the sand as fast as they could. Pancho was thrilled, bounding far ahead and rolling around then coming back to join them. It was dark now and the only light was the head torch on Marco's head, jumping about as he moved.

"Where are we going, Marco?" Rosalita asked, gasping for breath.

"Just run, Mariposa, keep running!"

A light flashed in the distance. Marco stepped up his pace, clearly familiar with the terrain. Rosalita and Hal, still weak from their captivity, staggered along after him. They weaved through the desert shrubs, with Pancho zigzagging along beside them.

Within a couple of minutes it became clear where they were heading. A row of red lights led into the distance. It was a makeshift airstrip and at the end of it a plane – it looked tiny but, prayed Hal, hopefully just about big enough for the three of them and Pancho to fit in.

After a final sprint they all bundled into plane's side door. Rosalita and Hal slumped into the back seats. With Pancho on top of them it was very tight, but neither of them cared. No ropes. No gags. No psychos with neon teeth. It was luxury compared to the cave.

Marco sat in front with the pilot, a lean faced man with greying blond hair. He was in his early 60s like Marco and had a strong American accent.

"How's it hanging, Señor Marco?" he shouted. "Crazy Hawk Alabama at your service as agreed. Are y'all set for the mountains?"

"Thanks Crazy Hawk," said Marco. "I really owe you, old friend."

"Where are we going?" shouted Rosalita.

"Somewhere nobody will find us," said Marco, laughing. "You thought Pretty Boy's cave was secret. Just wait till you see the Sierra Madre Occidental mountains."

"Sure thing," shouted Crazy Hawk. "It's the true boondocks. Home to the Tarahumara Indians, some of the most private people on earth. "

The plane began to trundle down the runway and pick up speed.

"We'll have time to make a plan there," shouted Marco above the noise of the engine. "Get Hal back to his family." He smiled at Rosalita. "As for us, Mariposa, we'll need to keep our heads down for a while."

Hal looked over at Rosalita. Her whole face had changed. She had the bruise above her left eye and a couple of cuts, but there was something else different about her. To Hal, she had always looked so uptight and sour, but now she looked relaxed, free. Like a huge burden had lifted from her. "Blissed out" to use his dad's words.

Rosalita smiled at Hal as she stroked Pancho, who was dozing half on his lap, half on hers. She even gave the panting dog a quick kiss.

"Well *cabroncito*," she said, putting her head on Hal's shoulder. "Thanks to Marco rescuing us, I didn't have to waste my three pesos on you after all."

PART THREE

The Sun Queen

Hands steady, eyes unblinking, Sol lifted the pistol: a Smith and Wesson Model 41. It was an old-fashioned weapon with a long, heavy muzzle. Sol relished the way it handled, like something a cowboy might use, or even a pirate.

The Sun Queen, as all the newspapers now called Sol, breathed in deep, adjusted her sunglasses, spread her feet and, perfectly balanced, took aim. Oh, how she loved guns, and after years of firing at all sorts of targets, she had become a deadly shot.

Her target this time was a mango, but its location was unusual. It was perched on the bald, sweaty head of Luis Ramírez, the policeman who had arrested her father five years ago. Now, here was the veteran cop in front of her, scared out of his brains and tied to a palm tree. For Sol, this was a day of sweet revenge.

Tomas Ceto, guarded by a posse of thuggish hit men, admired his daughter from the comfort of a deck chair. He felt fully back in control at his new hideaway on the outskirts of the Chihuahua Desert. Here, he was king once again, not only of his staff, but nature itself, judging by the perfect lawn which stretched around him neat and flat as a pool table.

The Toad smiled as Sol cocked her head to one side, ready to fire her pistol towards the roped policeman.

"What a girl," he thought, "she does me proud, unlike that traitorous minx Mariposa."

Sol stood directly in front of her victim, her finger tight on the pistol's trigger. The policeman was dripping with sweat, making every effort to keep the mango on his head still.

"We should call you Candle Man," taunted Sol. "Look at you, melting like hot wax."

Sol smiled, reveling in her power; she loved taunting her father's enemies.

"Don't worry, baldy, this gun may be old but it's lethal." Sol narrowed her dark eyes. "I never miss."

A shot rang out: the mango exploded. Some parrots in a nearby coconut palm squawked and flew up in in a flash of green and red. Sol grinned as Luis Ramírez slumped against his ropes, dizzy with relief that he had not been hit.

"What a sorry sight you are, Señor Ramírez." Sol turned a tap beside her and a garden sprinkler burst to life, fanning the policeman with water. "That will cool you down, you're sweating like a mule."

"Great shot, Sol darling," shouted Tomas Ceto from the top of the lawn. "Bravo!"

El Sapo had been waiting for this moment, waiting to watch Luis Ramírez squirm. He sat back, basking in his new freedom and stroking his grey moustache in a hand-held mirror. Oh yes, thought Tomas Ceto, as he admired his reflection. I rather like my moustache now it has turned grey, makes me look noble, aristocratic.

In reality much of the last five years had been a breeze for *El Sapo*. The prison guards had treated the famous gangster well – knowing he had contacts that would hurt them at the drop of a hat if they laid a finger on him.

Yet, in other ways, Tomas Ceto did really look older now, his face haggard, his back stooped, his belly, big as a basketball, straining against his belt. The Toad put his physical decline, indeed all the stress in his life, down to one thing and one thing only: Mariposa.

He had at first been overjoyed by his Little Butterfly's miraculous recovery at the hands of some of Mexico's finest doctors and plastic surgeons. They had treated her in a secret clinic deep in the far south of the country, in the jungles of Yucatán, where he, Sol, Mariposa and Marco had all fled immediately following the fateful birthday shootout in Mexico City.

And yet, once Mariposa's surgery was over six months later, the drug lord had struggled to look his daughter in the face, cope with her scars. It got worse, as his Little Butterfly now realized exactly what her 'Papi' did for a living.

Oh yes, thought Tomas Ceto sadly, Mariposa soon stood up to him, blamed him for her wounds, even called him a 'madman', a 'bloodthirsty maniac'. The Toad winced at the memory, it was too much to take. Mariposa so angry, so rude, his sweet, obedient butterfly transformed into something else entirely, something he really didn't like at all.

One night was particularly awful to recall for Tomas Ceto, when he had shouted at his wife, Carmen. Mariposa had lept to her mother's defense and hit her Papi square in his big belly. Outraged –no one ever hit *El Sapo*! –he had slapped his Little Butterfly. The drug lord yelled at her to leave and never come back.

Mariposa spat at her father and walked out, with Marco –on Tomas Ceto's instructions –in hot pursuit. Using false identities the odd-looking pair turned up at *Miracles in Hell* the following day after the 35-hour bus ride to the Tex-Mex border. The Pastor immediately provided Rosalita and her 'Uncle Marco' a new home.

The following week a squad of gun-wielding Special Forces led by Luis Ramírez swooped in and arrested the surprised drug lord at his hideaway. Sol was held down, screaming, as Tomas Ceto was driven away in handcuffs. Sol swore revenge on her little sister, convinced it was Mariposa who had tipped off the law of their father's whereabouts.

Many thought *El Sapo* would be finished once he was behind bars, but; far from it. His critics hadn't realized the devotion of his greatest ally, Sol, the power hungry teenager with the sun tattoos, who was destined to take on her Papi's criminal empire and never look back. And sure enough, five years later once security had slackened, an elite squad of men loyal to Tomas Ceto sprung him out of his prison cell: an ingenious plan of Sol's, using bribery, brute force and a laundry basket.

Oh, yes, mused The Toad, puffing up a plume of cigar smoke. *Pretty Boy Sánchez can keep my disloyal Little Butterfly, I'm not paying a peso for her. I have my Sun Queen now and even better, she is about to scare the living daylights out of the cop who arrested me. I'm back,* he told himself as he watched Sol reload her pistol, *the most feared man in Mexico once more.*

*

"Sol," Tomas Ceto shouted, stubbing out his cigar with his fingers. "Come here, my darling, I have something for you."

Sol sashayed across the lawn in her black military-style jumpsuit, pistol still in her hand. She certainly had her mother's good looks, The Toad thought: she was a dead-ringer for his wife, Carmen, in her twenties. But, thank goodness, Sol had got his strength, his power. Carmen could never handle his line of work, hadn't got the stomach for it, a complete bag of nerves.

"What's up, Papi?" asked Sol. She had called her father Papi ever since Mariposa had left. "Shall I put another mango on top of Luis Ramírez?"

Tomas Ceto gestured to a mound of strawberries in a bowl in front of him. He plucked one out.

"Why don't you use one of these next," *El Sapo* said, dipping the strawberry into a silver jug of cream. He laughed. "The cream will help it stick to his head."

He picked up an assault rifle, fitted with a huge telescopic sight, lying at his feet.

"As you know, my dear, this is a Kalashnikov," Tomas Ceto said, smearing gun oil along its magazine. "Part rifle, part machine gun. Designed by a Russian soldier. Over 50 years old and still the world's most used assault rifle. So simple, so timeless...so lethal."

The drug lord nodded in admiration and sniffed at the gun's barrel. "It has killed millions of people. Imagine being responsible for creating something that has caused such destruction, my love. Millions!" He smiled. "One more won't hurt."

Sol nodded in approval, exchanged the pistol for the rifle, and picked up the cream-dipped strawberry. She walked back to the policeman, who stood miserably tugging against his ropes, blinking sweat from his eyes. She placed the strawberry carefully on his head.

"Take care, Señor Ramírez," Sol said, her face inches from his. "I can shoot a flea off a cow's tail but..." She placed her thumb in the center of the cop's forehead. "Any sudden moves and, oops, the bullet could go anywhere."

"Please, don't do this," said Luis Ramírez quietly. Considering his grim situation the policeman was showing great dignity. "I have a wife and three children. Don't you have any heart at all?"

"Not for the cop who arrested my father," said Sol, briskly. "Never!"

Sol paced back fifty yards with the weapon and lay belly down on the grass. She lined up the gun, tweaking its sights with the precision of a safe cracker and took aim. Some magpies shrieked and chattered in the bushes behind them. Luis Ramírez closed his eyes, sweat pouring off him, bracing himself for the inevitable.

Fzzzt!

The bullet thudded into the palm tree behind him, the strawberry blasted to smithereens. The policeman slumped down once more in a combination of relief and shock. Tomas Ceto cheered from the sidelines.

"What next, you lunatic?" Luis Ramírez called out to the drug lord. "A cherry, a peanut."

"What a good idea!" said Sol, standing up. "But let me see, oh dear." She pouted her lips, her voice childlike. "It's lunch soon and I want a quick swim. So, no more time to play I'm afraid." She shrugged. "Sorry, Señor Ramírez."

Sol lifted the rifle to her hip and fired another bullet, this time into the grass inches from Luis Ramírez's feet. Sol laughed as she watched him flinch in fear.

"That was for you Papi," Sol shouted across the lawn to Tomas Ceto. "Pay back for locking you up all those years."

Minutes later Sol was swimming up and down the villa's pool, the water a startling blue. She didn't seem to have a care in the world. Behind her, far across the immaculate lawn, Luis Ramírez watched her, still slumped against his ropes.

The Sun Queen swam over a hundred lengths, graceful as a mermaid, then dried off and sat back on a sun lounger. Here, she sipped a glass of champagne in her swimsuit, regularly topped up for her by one of her father's white-suited flunkies.

Sol let the champagne swirl deliciously around her mouth and stretched back. Oh, this shooting is thirsty work, she thought to herself. She smiled and closed her eyes, falling into a deep, contented sleep.

*

"Wake up, Sol!"

The Sun Queen sat bolt upright on the lounger as if jolted by an electric shock. She grabbed for her pistol.

"Steady, my darling." Tomas Ceto was standing over her. "It's only me."

"Sorry Papi," said Sol, putting down the weapon. "I must have nodded off. What's up?"

"It's your sister." *El Sapo*'s voice was urgent. "She and Marco are no longer on our radar." He shook his head in frustration. "Pretty Boy couldn't've hurt them –he hasn't got his ransom yet. They must be somewhere so remote there's no signal. Or else Mariposa's bug has been removed..."

"But Mariposa didn't even know we bugged her," interrupted Sol, annoyed that The Little Butterfly was causing trouble again. "She had no idea the microchip was hidden in her necklace." Sol shrugged. "And why hasn't Marco been in contact? He's supposed to be keeping us posted."

"That's what's worrying me," said Tomas Ceto, frowning. "The last signal they were in Sierra Madre mountains then it went dead."

The Toad gestured towards the horizon. "Why would Pretty Boy want to go to the mountains, he's a city slicker? The fool must have lost her." Tomas Ceto dragged hard on a cigar. "And maybe Mariposa's escaped Marco too. Looks like the Little Butterfly has slipped all her nets." He threw his half-smoked cigar into the pool: "But she won't slip mine."

*

Sol put on a bathrobe over her swimsuit and hurried after her Papi who was descending the stairs into the basement of the villa. They continued down a corridor flanked with armed guards and finally into a dimly lit room filled with computers, their screens flickering wildly.

"No sign of Mariposa, Señor Ceto," said a young, shorthaired women tapping at a keyboard. " The signal is still lost."

"Oh, Little Butterfly," said *El Sapo*, not without a hint of pride. "You were always the smart one."

Sol bristled at these words. She watched the digital map in front of her praying for a sign of Mariposa –but there was no blip, no movement. Clearly her sister was well and truly off the radar.

So Mariposa has outsmarted Pretty Boy and maybe Marco, Sol thought, *well, so what, she will never outsmart me.* She had been waiting for an excuse to get revenge on that traitor, her little sister, for years now.

"Don't worry, Papi," said Sol, standing behind her father as he anxiously

113

watched the computer screen. She towered over him, massaging his hunched shoulders. "I'll take some men and track down Mariposa. I'm good in the mountains. We need to find her before Pretty Boy." She sighed. "We won't hurt her, just catch her and bring her back."

"She certainly has a lot of explaining to do," said *El Sapo*. He smiled at Sol. "But I might be ready to forgive the Little Butterfly. She must have learned her lesson by now, don't you think? Might want to come home to Papi after all this time. Say sorry."

Sol tensed, her heart still sour at the mention of her sister, but her face remained calm. She had worked so hard to win her father's respect, to become The Sun Queen. Never would she let the Little Butterfly de-throne her again.

"Yes, it might be nice to have Mariposa back, Papi," Sol lied, grinning, as she turned to leave the room. But whether I return her dead or alive, she thought to herself, remains to be seen.

"Wait a minute, boss, look at this!" The woman working on the computer shouted out. She was thudding away at her keyboard like a crazed pianist. "Here, look!" A red dot appeared on the digital map in front of her, flashing steady as a heartbeat. "There she is, that's Mariposa! She's back!"

"Thank God," said Tomas Ceto, calmly eyeing the screen.

"Let me go after her, Papi!" pleaded Sol.

The drug lord rubbed his moustache for a long time, as if thinking through a chess move, then winked at his eldest daughter.

"Ok, my dear," he said fondly. "I'll give you two of my best men." He flicked his fingers at a pair of dark uniformed bruisers standing nearby. "Bring Mariposa home to me."

"I will Papi, you can count on me."

Once Tomas Ceto had left the room, Sol's eyes lit up as she touched the digital map in front of her. She traced her thumb across the remote Sierra Madre Occidental mountains to the point where the bug stopped pulsing – a little town by the name of Creel.

"*Creel,*" Sol read from an information box that had just pinged up on screen.

"*Population 5000. Town in the heart of Mexico's Copper Canyon, home to the Tarahumara Indians. The Tarahumara are thought to be among the best long distance runners in the world, a tribal people so remote that some still live in caves.*"

"But not remote enough for me, little sister," thought Sol, still transfixed by the flashing dot. "Poor Little Butterfly, you can fly but you can't hide."

Squirrel Soup
Unknown location, Copper Canyon

Hal and Rosalita sniffed at the meaty broth in the bowls in front of them.

"Never had squirrel soup for breakfast, guys?" Crazy Hawk Alabama asked, throwing his head back and roaring with laughter. "Lovely stuff. Very nutritious."

Hal lifted the bowl to his lips and cautiously took a sip: "Tasty," he said, smiling at Blanca, the Tarahumara Indian lady in a pink dress who had just cooked it for him. "Tell her it's very tasty, Crazy Hawk."

It actually tasted worse than The Pastor's cow-gut soup but Hal didn't want to offend. He realized he wasn't going to get Crunchy Nut Cornflakes and a fresh croissant in the middle of the Sierra Madre Mountains.

Hal, Rosalita, Marco and Crazy Hawk were all sitting cross-legged around a wood fire as Blanca topped up their bowls. Rosalita wasn't squeamish at all. She glugged back her liquefied squirrel as if it was chocolate milkshake.

"Get it down you, *cabroncito*," she whispered to Hal. "So what if it's a tree rat. It's an honor to be offered meat by the Tarahumaras. They mostly eat veg." She winked. "And hunger is the best sauce, right?"

She was right. Hal was starving. Neither he nor Rosalita had eaten anything since their escape.

What an escape it had been too. After shaking off Pretty Boy, Crazy Hawk Alabama had flown the little Skyhawk to a remote airstrip lit only by the moon beside an immense canyon. They had left the plane in a shed-like hangar and walked for miles across the dry, rocky hills, coyotes howling in the distance, until they reached the home of Blanca, a friend of Crazy Hawk. She had provided them blankets and hammocks and they slept like gypsies under the stars until the morning sun woke them - along with the smell of squirrel soup.

During the night Hal had been so tired he had barely taken in his new surroundings. Now it was light, it was clear that Blanca lived in a seriously weird place: to Hal it looked more suited to hobbits and unicorns than human beings.

It was basically a cave, decided Hal, well, not even a cave, more a nook under an outcrop of rock with the bonus of a pretty view of a lake and a small waterfall. The nook was full of tools, saucepans, strung up washing and piles of sweet corn. It was damp and smelled like bonfires and yet to Hal and Rosalita, it was heaven after Pretty Boy's garage.

And how good it felt to be free; Hal couldn't really believe it. One minute a gun stuck to his head, the next saved by Marco the Narco, then whisked away by Crazy Hawk Alabama and now eating squirrel served by a smiling Tarahumara in a pink dress.

As for Rosalita, she had been transformed, her once rock hard face now soft and flushed as she chatted. Having ripped off his fake wart, Marco seemed a far friendlier soul too and Pancho was as relaxed as ever, lying at Hal's feet, enjoying the heat of the fire.

A Tarahumara boy ran into the cave – Blanca's grandson. He was in his late teens and wore a red poncho and sandals made out of leather. He looked super fit and carried a bow and arrow in one hand and a dead squirrel in the other.

"Hey Gabriel, how's it going?" asked Crazy Hawk. The boy's face lit up with a smile when he saw the old pilot. "Unlike most kids here, Gabriel's still as skilled with a bow and arrow as his ancestors. And as fast! You're running in that big race down in Creel today, aren't you, boy?"

Gabriel nodded, his breath smoking in the cool morning air. "American runners race us," Gabriel said, struggling with his English. "I see them already. They wear funny rubber clothes. Very tight."

"You crack me up, Gabriel," said Crazy Hawk. "That rubber is called Lycra. Clothing so tight it makes your voice go high. *La, la, laaaa!*" Crazy Hawk winced as his voice broke on the high note. "I'm like you, Gabriel, give me a poncho to run in any day."

He winked at Hal and Rosalita. "The Tarahumara are some of the best long distance runners in the world. It's in their blood." He puffed out his chest. "And it's my honor to run with them."

"You run too, Crazy Hawk?" chided Rosalita, "at your age!"

"Don't mince your words Rosi," he replied, laughing. "Oh, hell yes, I love to run but I'm young compared to some of the Tarahumara, a few still do regular marathons in their 70s."

"Now that's impressive." Rosalita nodded in approval.

"The Tarahumara call me Zigzag," Crazy Hawk added. "It's because I run in zigzags – especially after a bit of corn beer." He laughed. "Once you have a Tarahumara nickname you are one of the family. The running bonds you."

He smiled at Blanca, who was using a penknife to skin the squirrel Gabriel had brought her.

"Crazy Hawk has lived among the Tarahumara for years," explained Marco, punching his friend on the arm. "He eats their recipes, speaks their lingo and delivers their medicines in his plane." Marco wagged a finger at Hal. "Don't be fooled by him though, he may look like a scrawny old buzzard, but he can still run 50 kilometers non-stop over these hills, no sweat."

"50 kilometers!" Hal choked on his soup.

"That's why I don't wear Lycra," said Crazy Hawk. "Running over that distance in rubber shorts my butt would turn blue."

Hal and Rosalita burst out laughing. This set off Blanca, even though she didn't understand a word.

"To be honest I'm no real runner," said Crazy Hawk, pointing at Gabriel. "But this boy is. They call him *El Venado*, the deer, he's that fast. He can run twice the distance I can. Up to 100 kilometers in one go."

"100 kilometers!" said Rosalita. "Come on! Is that even possible?"

"Sure it is, remember the Tarahumaras are born to run," said Crazy Hawk, his thin face lit up. "It's what they do. They run across the hills, village to village, from an early age. They don't run to win races or get fit or look skinny. Just do it because they love it!"

"OK, OK," Marco cut in, clapping his hands. "Enough about running. We can watch Gabriel race the Americans later. We all need a bit of time to relax." He gestured at the craggy landscape. "No way Pretty Boy is going to find us here."

"Marco," said Hal. "I must call my parents."

"Of course you must, Ginger," replied Marco, pushing himself away from the fire. "There's no signal here but you can send them a message from Creel later. But don't give our location. Just say you are safe. Once Pretty Boy knows where one of us is, he knows where all of us are."

Marco looked over at Rosalita, who was now slurping down her third bowl of squirrel soup.

"And you have to decide if you want to see your family, Mariposa," he said. "Your dad? Sol? I will help reunite you if you want me to." He softened his voice. "But if you want to hide from them, I'll protect you too. Your choice."

"I don't want to see either of them ever again," said Rosalita without a second's thought. "They are not my family anymore." She gestured to Marco. "You are." Then, as an afterthought. "And my mum, wherever she is."

*

After breakfast, Crazy Hawk sniffed at his armpits, announced that he 'stunk like a coyote' and needed to wash. Hal, Rosalita, Marco, Gabriel and Pancho all followed him as he zigzagged down the slope to the lakeside at a blistering pace.

Once everyone had stripped to their swim gear behind various pine trees, they tiptoed along the lake's edge before plunging into the freezing water. Rosalita squealed with delight as Gabriel and Hal splashed her. To escape she dived underwater, popping up like a seal beneath the waterfall. With her long dark hair and big smile, for a second Hal thought he was seeing Gina Moreno again.

After dashing up and down the side of the lake barking at the swimmers, Pancho jumped up on to a boulder. He teetered briefly on the edge before sploshing in beside Gabriel and Rosi. He circled them, slick as a giant otter, occasionally lifting his nose and snorting happily.

Some orange butterflies fluttered above them. Hal wondered if the butterflies were the ones his dad wanted to film. Wow, he thought, that all seemed like a million years ago. He really must contact his dad from Creel, he'd be worried sick and as for his mum, she got weepy watching *The Simpsons* let alone her son getting kidnapped by Pretty Boy Sánchez…

With Hal lost in dreams of home, Gabriel and Rosalita continued splashing and ducking each other while Crazy Hawk and Marco washed in the shallows before stretching out on a boulder to dry. After a while Gabriel said farewell and dashed away to get to his race.

"I'm so happy, Hal," said Rosalita. The two teenagers were floating on their backs on the lake, blinking into the morning sun, as Pancho paddled around them. Some birds chirruped in the trees on the shore.

"Gabriel was lovely," she sighed. "Most boys are scared of me, can't look at me. But Gabriel didn't seem to notice my scars at all."

"That's cool, Rosi," said Hal. He felt ashamed of all the names he'd called her back in Pretty Boy's garage. After a pause, he spat a jet of water at her to lighten the mood. "But, trust me," he said. "You'll scare poor Gabriel to pieces once he gets to know you properly."

"Ahh, you little *cabroncito*," Rosalita laughed and pushed Hal's head underwater. Once they'd wrestled for a while they joined Crazy Hawk and Marco drying on their boulder.

"So how do you two know each other?" Rosalita asked the old friends. She leant back against a nearby pine tree using her Jeans as a pillow.

"We met here in the Sierra Madre, Rosi," said Crazy Hawk, flicking a fly off his shoulder. "It was years ago now. Marco came here as a hideaway before he started working for your father."

"It's such a magic place this Copper Canyon," said Marco, a far away look in his eyes. "It's even deeper than the Grand Canyon in parts you know." He stretched his arms wide. "But now the Tarahumara are in trouble…the big companies are using the land for gold mining and cutting down the trees for timber. Even worse, people like Pretty Boy are forcing some of the locals to grow drugs rather than corn. Some villages are near starving." He nodded his head. "Crazy Hawk made me see the horror of drugs, the side effects on completely innocent people."

Marco stopped and looked up at Hal and Rosalita. The two teenagers were both hooked by his description of the beautiful, dangerous, fragile new world around them.

"Remember I was born into nothing," said Marco, shrugging. "A Juárez street kid. You know that, Rosi. My time with the Tarahumara and this old fool here…" He pointed to Crazy Hawk. "Well, it really changed me. Oh, I was a bad man, still am really, but I'm way better than I was."

"Yes, you were a real badass when I met you," said Crazy Hawk, putting an arm around Marco's shoulders. "No question about that. And yes, you are still an ugly brute now." He paused and smiled. "But I'm very proud to call you my friend."

It fell silent, all four of the bathers lost in their own thoughts. A fish jumped high and then plopped back into the water near the edge of the lake. The air smelled of pine trees and Pancho's damp coat.

Rosalita looked at her wrist. "Mamma Mia, the time!" She showed her watch to the others. "We need to get to Creel fast or we'll miss the start of Gabriel's race."

"Hurray," shouted Hal, running back towards the cave. "I can finally call home!"

Running Wild

Back at Blanca's cave, Crazy Hawk pulled down a tarpaulin, revealing two beat-up Suzuki quad bikes. With Hal and Pancho on the back of his bike and Rosalita riding with Marco on the other, they raced towards Creel, bouncing over rocks and skidding through dirt and sand, before finally hitting the tarmac road that led to the outskirts of town.

Soon they were among the race crowds milling about near the town center. The Tarahumara women stood out in their yellow, red and pink ponchos, ready to cheer on their sons and husbands, and a few to compete in the race themselves. As the bikes revved closer Hal and Marco could make out Gabriel. He was with a group of Tarahumara youths all dressed in traditional ponchos and leather running sandals.

"Great you are here," said Gabriel, as Crazy Hawk and Hal pulled up alongside him. "Now, try this." Gabriel handed over a leather gourd to Hal. "We call it *tesgüino*, corn beer. It good. Good for body, for heart. You try, friend, just little bit. "

Hal smiled and glugged back a sip of the *tesgüino*, choking horribly.

"Good, yes?"

Hal, his eyes watering, gave Gabriel a thumbs-up even though the drink tasted like a bad chemistry experiment.

"Fermented corn beer is a Tarahumara secret weapon, a sacred drink," said Crazy Hawk. "In small amounts it gives them stamina, fuels them." He laughed. "And gives them a headache when they drink too much." He chugged several times on the gourd. "I love the stuff."

"Hey, look at those American runners," said Rosalita, pointing at a group of skinny, Lycra clad men and women near the race starting line.

Several of the runners were leaning against railings and stretching their muscly limbs, others were rubbing gel into the calves, one blonde woman was jogging up and down punching the air and another in a BORN TO RUN baseball cap and leopard skin tights was sitting cross-legged in a yoga pose chanting to herself. They all looked very focused on the race.

In contrast the Tarahumara runners seemed to be having a ball, swigging on corn beer, laughing, chatting. No stretching, no energy bars and not a yoga move in sight.

"Tarahumara runners aren't big on warming up," explained Crazy Hawk. "They run all the time but rarely get injured. Running for them is like driving a car for us, it's instinctive, part of them, whatever the terrain. Well, some of them but not all. " He gestured to a group overweight Tarahumaras in jeans and T-shirts who had come to support rather than run.

"Some Tarahumaras living near Creel have got soft and fat, lost the old ways. They watch too much TV and eat fast food. It's really only the ones deep in the Sierra Madre who are still super fit." He smiled. "The race today is 100 kilometers, not sure some of those guys would make 100 yards. But you can't blame them for wanting another life - living in caves is tough."

Blanca appeared with a running number pinned to her chest. Everyone gave her a cheer. Hal couldn't believe it. This tiny, sun wrinkled granny was going to race 100 kilometers, still dressed in her pink dress and carrying a big wooden stick – and she'd just cooked them all breakfast! Blanca took a swig of corn beer and gave Crazy Hawk a smile. She was ready to go.

"Let's do it, Blanca!" said Crazy Hawk, who was ready to run too, now dressed in a white poncho and sandals.

The nearby Americans runners, all decked out in flash trainers were still gearing themselves up. Hal smiled at the leopard skin yoga woman. She was now bending one of her legs over her head. Hal thought she'd need a spanner to get it back again.

"Good luck to you, guys," Crazy Hawk shouted across to them. "Not many Americans brave the Sierra Madre these days, it's good to see y'all." The Lycra clad athletes waved back, giving the Tarahumara runners thumbs up signs.

"Sure thing, brother, all the best to you guys too" said the yoga woman to Marco. She gave Crazy Hawk a peace sign. "This place rocks, man. Great energy. Loving the aura."

She looks like she's loving the aura, thought Hal, whatever aura is.

A voice on the loud speaker wished everyone good luck and told them to move to the starting line. It went quiet as the 30-odd runners shuffled forward, then there was a shout, a cheer and they were off. Blanca speed-walked away at a furious pace propelled by her stick, Crazy Hawk jogging by her side. Gabriel dashed ahead amongst the leading huddle of Tarahumaras and Americans, including leopard pants.

Hal and Rosalita cheered wildly, with Pancho barking in confusion. "Go Gabriel! Go Blanca! Go Crazy Hawk."

"I'm not Crazy Hawk today," shouted the pilot. "I'm Zigzag."

"Go Zigzag," they shouted, and he really did zigzag, noticed Hal, whether due to corn beer or running style, he wasn't sure.

With no breeze whipping up dust, the bright-colored runners were visible far into the distance, the sky a cloudless blue. Hal watched until they were out of sight then turned to Marco but he'd vanished. Hal really needed to call his parents now. He wasn't sure how to ride the quad bike so he'd have to walk. It was only a few minutes to the town center.

"I must call Mum and Dad, Rosalita," he said. But when he turned she was no longer by his side either. "Rosi?"

"Why don't you join me instead, Hal," said a silky voice behind him. It was the human equivalent of a cat purring, or maybe a tiger. "My name is Sol."

A gun barrel prodded hard into Hal's lower back.

*

Hal tried to turn around but Sol lifted the gun up to his neck and increased its pressure.

"Don't even think about it, ginger man."

Hal was tempted to tell Sol she sounded just like her sister but thought it would be a bad idea. Out of the corner of his eye he could see a man in a black uniform behind Rosalita. She had a gun in her back too.

When will this ever end? Hal thought. Will I ever get home? And where on earth was Marco?

Every time Hal asked Sol a question about where they were going, she jabbed the gun even harder into his back and told him to shut up. He was forced to obey.

They weaved through the edge of the crowds to the main street leading to Creel's center. Sol expertly steered Hal, smiling at any passers-by to avoid suspicion.

Once in the town square, Sol jerked Hal along a side street then down a dirt drive leading into a big, deserted, stone building, partly painted white. It also had a cross on its door: Hal realized it was some sort of chapel.

Marco was already sitting on a pew to the front of the building under a small, stained glass window decorated with saints and angels. Hal smiled despite his fear: Marco was no saint, and certainly no angel.

When Marco looked up at Hal his face was like a mask. No wink or sign of recognition. Whose side are you on Marco? Hal thought. He was about to get his answer.

"Ah, well done Sol, you've found them," Marco said. He smiled approvingly. "I've set up Skype with your father. The reception's good here. He's ready to speak to Mariposa."

"Here she comes now," said Sol, as the man in the black uniform shoved Mariposa into the little church. Hal tried to catch her eye but she had been gagged and blindfolded. What was Marco playing at? Who was he helping now? Hal felt worn out: these people were doing his head in.

Marco propped up a laptop on the church's altar table and an instantly recognizable face flashed up on screen.

"Hello, my Little Butterfly," said Tomas Ceto. The drug lord was sitting by a swimming pool, a cigar in his hand and a bogey-green cocktail balanced on his enormous belly.

"Let me get a good look at you, Mariposa," said *El Sapo*. "It's been a long time." Marco shifted the laptop towards Mariposa, who was now slumped next to him on the front pew of the church.

"Oh, there she is!" said *El Sapo*. "There's my Little Butterfly. How I've missed you."

Hal could see Mariposa wrestling with her tied hands and moaning horribly against her gag. Behind her, Sol smirked at her discomfort. Hal's heart went out to his fellow prisoner – she really did have the family from hell.

"Please take the gag off her, Marco," said Tomas Ceto. "I want to hear my Little Butterfly say sorry. Want her to come home to her Papi."

Another man in black –a near twin of the man who had captured Mariposa– pulled out a knife from his belt and cut the ropes from Mariposa's hands and mouth. Once free, the Little Butterfly stayed silent. Hal looked across at his friend. The Rosalita of the last few days, the gentle, light hearted, funny one, had gone. Her eyes were once again blank and cold. This was not going to end well.

"So, what have you got to tell me, Mariposa?" Tomas Ceto said. "Are you ready to come home to Papi? To say sorry?"

Rosalita said nothing, she looked at the screen, her face neutral.

"Oh, so it's the silent treatment is it?" Tomas Ceto peered towards the laptop. "I see you still have the butterfly necklace I gave you all those years ago. And I hear you have some butterfly tattoos. That must mean you still love me really."

Mariposa looked at him, her face a mask.

"You have to understand Mariposa," said *El Sapo*, inhaling on his cigar. "I am a big man in Mexico. I pay for schools and hospitals to be built along the border." He shrugged his shoulders. "The Mexican government doesn't do this, so I have to. I have to help the poor and the people love me for it. They even sing folk songs about me."

"They don't love you," said Rosalita quietly. "They are *terrified* of you."

"Oh Mariposa, that is not true," said Tomas Ceto, an edge to his voice now. "I help the community. I employ lots of people, provide work for poor families…"

"But only as gangsters and drug dealers," Mariposa interrupted. "Who get killed doing your dirty work, or who die if they refuse. You destroy everything you touch." She was warming up now, her voice hard and clear. "And you don't do it to help the poor, you monster, but for the money." She spat at the laptop. "Always the money. You are a fake, Papi, a coward and a fake!"

"Mariposa! Stop it." *El Sapo* zoomed close up to the screen, his bulbous face enraged. "Stop it! You cannot speak to me like this. I was just carrying on the family business. What choice did I have? I wanted to make my father proud, do my duty…"

"What duty?" shouted Rosalita. "A duty to kill people! Good job, Dad. Just a shame you didn't save any duty for your wife, your daughters…"

"But, Mariposa, all that money I made paid for your toys, your education, your childhood…"

"A childhood where I got shot," Mariposa yelled back. "Thanks for that."

Hal caught a glimpse of Sol. She was trying not to smile, clearly loving all this, her Papi and Mariposa at war again.

"As we are in a church and you clearly think you are God." Rosalita was really on a roll now. "I'd like to make a confession." She glowered at her father. "I hate you, Papi, I hate you more than anyone on earth! I wanted to love you, believe in you, that's why I kept the necklace, the tattoos. But you let me down every time." She shrugged. "Let yourself down."

With this, she ripped the butterfly necklace from her neck and threw it at the laptop. "I would rather die than come home to you. In fact…" She shook her fist at the laptop, "I am ashamed to be your daughter!"

Tomas Ceto stared at his Little Butterfly in disbelief. There was a long silence. Hal hardly dared breathe. *El Sapo* moved towards the screen, his eyes cold and fierce.

"Gag her Marco!" shouted the drug lord. "Gag her tight and bring her back to me." He looked across at Hal. "Then kill the boy."

"Are you sure, boss?" said Marco, reaching for his pistol. It was a slim model with a silencer attached.

"Yes, kill him," *El Sapo* nodded his head. "He's of no use to us." Hal felt his guts go south.

"Ok, then, but just before I do," said Marco, inspecting his silencer. His movements calm and slow as he pointed the gun towards Hal. "I'd just like you to know," he smiled at *El Sapo*, "that I'm deeply ashamed…" he swung the gun towards the laptop, "to call you my boss."

"Marco, what did you say, Marco…"

Marco fired into the laptop, instantly destroying Tomas Ceto's face, cigar and cocktail. Quick as a flash Marco fired a second shot into the leg of one of the black uniformed guards, who collapsed in agony. Before he could fire again the second guard kicked Marco's gun out of his hand and lashed at his face with his fist. The two men fell to the floor in a heap, grappling for the weapon.

The moment the first shot fired Rosalita tackled Sol who had been caught off guard by Marco's actions. The gun spun out of her hand, a bullet firing off and shattering the chapel's stained glass window, the various saints and angels dissolving, as if by magic, into a thousand tinkling fragments.

Rosalita hit Sol hard in the chest but The Sun Queen managed to deflect the punch and roll herself on top of her sister, locking Mariposa's neck against the floor with a forearm and pinning her arms down with her knees. Sol pressed down with all her might, Mariposa unable to budge. The younger sister was winded, gasping like a fish out of water.

Hal watched the unfolding scene in horror. One minute there was a Skyping session, next a gun pointed at him and now all hell had broken loose.

Hal knew he had to act fast: both Rosalita and Marco were in serious trouble. He needed a weapon. He looked around desperately. Up on the altar was a large, gold crucifix. "No, no, no," Hal whispered. "I can't use that!" His eyes darted from one suitable weapon to the next. The white altar candles (too soft), the wine chalice (too small), the communion table (too big). Then he heard Rosalita scream and knew he had no choice. He looked to the heavens, whispered 'sorry' then dashed towards the crucifix, skidding, then falling on the window's broken glass. From the floor, he glanced across at Rosalita. She was motionless under a now deranged-looking Sol, clearly enjoying throttling the life out of her hated sibling.

Hal levered himself back up and grabbed at the crucifix. He took hold of its wooden base and swung it with all his might at Sol. It smashed into the back of her head. Sol teetered for a couple of seconds then fell forward on top of Mariposa and rolled onto the church floor, out cold.

Hal looked over to Marco who had managed to overcome the second guard, gag him and was now tying his hands behind his back. The other guard was still clutching at his shot leg, moaning softly.

Rosalita sat up, her breath becoming calmer. Taking Hal's hand she pulled herself up on her feet and whispered: "Good job, tough guy. All we need for Sol now is some garlic and a sharp stake."

"Oh God, I pray I haven't hurt her too bad!" said Hal, looking down in terror at Sol's body. "She's still breathing isn't she?"

"Of course she is," said Rosalita. "Trust me, it would take much more than a tap on the head to finish my sister." She gave Hal a peck on the cheek. "Thank you, *cabroncito*."

"OK, you two, let's get out of here before anyone else turns up," ordered Marco. "I'm sorry this had to happen. Sol's arrival was a complete surprise and I had to go along with it. There was a bug in your necklace Mariposa." He lifted up the shattered orange butterfly to reveal the tiny digital device embedded in it. He then turned to Hal, smiling. "And sorry to point the gun at you, Ginger."

"I'm getting used to it," said Hal.

"Ok, let's get going," said Marco. "Head for the quad bikes, then we'll ride straight for the plane. It's no longer safe here."

Marco charged out of the chapel door, with Hal in hot pursuit holding Rosalita by the hand. She was still woozy from her scrap with Sol and needed a bit of support. Pancho, waiting outside the church door, barked happily on seeing them all again.

They tore down Creel's main street back to the Suzukis, dodging the few remaining race spectators. Marco straddled one of the bikes with Rosalita and Hal squeezing in behind him as best they could, Pancho on Hal's lap.

Marco fired up the ignition, the engine growled and the bike reared up on its two back wheels in a frenzy of dust before thudding down and hot-tailing back to the main road.

Flying Wild

Sol groaned and rubbed the back of her head. She pushed herself up on her knees on the church floor and quickly surveyed the scene – the smashed stained glass window, the crucifix at her side, one of her men whimpering with a bullet in his leg, the other bound and gagged. Hopeless fools! She'd deal with them later.

The Sun Queen rose to her feet and looked for her gun. She had three things on her mind and three things only: Mariposa, Marco and Hal, that stupid ginger fool who'd bashed her out cold. She could deal with her raging headache later, right now all she wanted was their blood, the whole blasted trio.

She picked up her pistol but it was jammed, kinked out of shape after smashing against the hard church floor. I'm really going to kill that ginger freak now, she swore, as she looked around for another weapon. All the guns were gone. And then she saw it in the church alcove: a wooden bow with several arrows on show as part of an exhibition about the Tarahumara. It was also a campaign: *"PRAY FOR THE TARAHUMARA"* read a sign. *"KEEP THE NARCOS OFF THEIR LAND!"* Sol shattered the glass display cabinet with her elbow and grabbed the bow, sticking three arrows in her belt. That will do fine, she decided, leaping over the crucifix.

Sol charged down the road, fast as a gazelle. She was a prize athlete who trained every day, running, shooting, boxing, karate; you name it, she did it. She knew her job, for all its perks, was dangerous and that she needed to be primed at all times. This was just the sort of situation she was 100 percent ready for and she was proud of it.

Sol could hear the revving of Marco's quad bike in the distance. She upped her pace sprinting full tilt with her head back, then stopped, squinting into the sun, marking out her target before running on.

Marco spotted Sol tearing towards them from way off. This is what he was trained for, too, and Sol was unmistakable as she chicaned through the crowds. It was clear to him she meant business, her blood was up. He swerved the bike off the main track onto a stretch of small, jagged rocks, the abrupt change in terrain nearly bouncing Pancho out of Hal's arms.

"Hang on tight," Marco shouted. "We've got company." Hal and Rosalita turned to see Sol, still running at them at a whirlwind pace. The Sun Queen pulled out her first arrow and threaded it through the bowstring. She stopped, totally focused, controlled her breathing, got down on one knee and took aim at the Suzuki, which was now bucking up along the rocks fifty yards away.

The first arrow whistled passed Rosalita's head by an inch and thudded against an olive tree behind the bike. Sol cursed, rose up and sprinted on towards them again, while threading her second arrow as she ran.

"Who does she think this is?" growled Marco, as Sol took aim again. "Pocahontas!"

The second arrow thudded into the side of the bike narrowly missing Marco. The elderly chauffeur didn't even flinch, just kept roaring on, his face in a tight-lipped, horizon-gazing trance.

By now they were gaining some ground but Sol's pursuit was relentless. For her third shot she didn't have time to crouch and stayed standing. She pulled the bow to its full arc, lifting it high and unleashed the final arrow.

Rosalita and Hal screamed as it soared towards them, putting their hands over their faces in a futile gesture of defense. The arrow thwacked down directly in front of the bike and shattered on the rocks, like a matchstick hit by a hammer. A second later and it would almost certainly have skewered one of them.

"Phew, thank goodness," said Hal, "looks like Pocahontas is out of arrows."

"Yes, but she's not out of anger," said Rosalita. "She'll keep after us I can guarantee. We need to get to that plane."

Marco kept revving the bike through the rocky landscape, furiously fighting with the handlebars as the bike reared and dipped. After a chilly start in the morning the sun was now fierce, with Pancho panting heavily on Hal's lap. Each of them swigged at a plastic barrel of water strapped to the bike's side.

After an hour of bone-jangling riding, the wooden hangar where Crazy Hawk housed his Skyhawk came into view and, seconds later, the vast canyon beyond it. Marco pulled up the bike in a swirl of red dust. Hal and Rosalita jumped off and made for the plane, Pancho at their heels.

"Can you fly, Marco?" Rosalita asked as they got into the plane.

"Crazy Hawk's given me a couple of lessons," he said, his voice full of confidence. "We'll be fine. The Cessna Skyhawk's an easy plane." They all bundled into the little four seater, Marco in the cockpit and once again Hal, Rosalita and Pancho squeezed in the rear. Marco fiddled around with the control panel for a minute or so and the engine spluttered into life.

"Thank God," said Marco, kissing the crucifix around his neck. "Crazy Hawk re-fuelled her last night. That guy is always ahead of the game."

In the distance Hal spotted another vehicle. It was some sort of futuristic Hummer with massive tires and mega-suspension. Oh no, thought Hal, please no. It was tearing along the boulder-strewn landscape as if it was Route 66, leaving a contrail of dust in its wake and making mincemeat of any obstacles. It would be on to them in no time.

"Marco, we've got company."

Hal could now make out who was in the speeding Hummer: Sol in the passenger seat with the wounded black-uniformed thug driving. The Sun Queen was leaning out of her window wrestling with some sort of machine gun that must have been stashed in the vehicle. No bows and arrows this time, thought Hal, Pocahontas is upping her game.

The little plane was now trundling along the runway, but the sandy strip was rugged and bumpy and her rock-eating Hummer was gaining pace.

"Don't panic," shouted Marco. "I'm gonna drop into the canyon before properly taking off, otherwise she'll kill us. We'll fall for a bit but it will be ok. Brace yourselves."

Before there was any time to protest Marco jerked the trembling plane away from the runway and towards the gaping chasm of the canyon. It was a void so deep the clouds were now sitting under them like a fluffy white safety blanket.

Sol's machine gun ripped open its first salvo behind them, one of the bullets pinging off the Cessna's tail, then they veered over the canyon's edge - falling. The passengers' hearts at once lurched from their bellies to their throats.

It was eerily quiet, the little plane plummeting fast through thick cloud. Hal's ears were popping like mad, Pancho yelping with anxiety beside him. Rosalita grabbed Hal's hand, both of them too scared to speak. It was like they were descending in a superfast, jittery elevator without the comfort of the big red STOP button.

More machine gun fire erupted from above. Come on Marco, fly us out of this, prayed Hal. Bullets whipped past them. They were beneath the cloud now, visibility returned. But Hal did not like what he saw: they were plummeting directly towards an outcrop of rust-colored rock.

Rosalita began to scream. Hal, sick with fear himself, held her hand, while holding down a quivering Pancho with his other. And then, like a dream, the plane leveled out as they swooped up through the sea of white.

Hal's stomach heaved as the Cessna continued its upward curve, before finally they burst through the low clouds back into the sunlight.

"Yeeeessss!" shouted Rosalita, her eyes looking around in awe as they soared free. "Now that's what I call a close shave!" She leant over and gave Hal a rib-crushing hug, both of them shaking with a combination of fear and adrenaline. Marco was laughing with relief in the cockpit.

"This is only my third flight ever," shouted Hal, above the noise of the straining engine. "But definitely the scariest. You never even demonstrated the safety procedures Marco. I mean, come on, where are the emergency exits, the oxygen masks..."

Rosalita laughed and grabbed onto Hal even harder.

In the distance Sol's turbo-boosted Hummer roared over the moonscape to the side of the canyon in a blaze of gold dirt, hot footing it back to Creel.

The Sun Queen was angry but far from defeated. Mariposa may have escaped and ripped off her necklace with the bug in it, but, Sol smiled, she was sure Hal hadn't noticed the bug she'd planted in the sole of his trainers. Her Papi would be able to give them Hal's whereabouts in no time. And that meant being able to track down her wretch of a sister and that traitorous snake Marco too.

*

The Cessna soared back over Creel, Marco pointing out a train pulling out of the town's station: the famous *El Chepe* that chugged its way through the towering rocks via a series of enormous, man made tunnels all the way to the Pacific Ocean.

Ten minutes later Marco gently dipped the plane down. "Look, there's Gabriel," he shouted, pointing down at a posse of runners below them. Gabriel was clearly visible in his white poncho. "He's near the middle of the pack, but they aren't half way yet, he'll turn up the gas later." Marco shrugged. "He's too young to win this time, but put some years on him and he'll be one of the greats." He smiled. "Anyway, 100 kilometers is a bit short for Gabriel, he'll be just getting warmed up."

"Where's Crazy Hawk and Blanca?" asked Rosalita.

"Oh, they'll be way back." Marco smiled. "But I guarantee you they will finish, they always do," he laughed, "and then Crazy Hawk will want to know where on earth his plane has gone."

"It such a wild place," said Hal, staring out at the landscape below him, "half of it looks dead, like nobody could survive here."

"Oh, you'd be surprised, Ginger," said Marco, leaning back. "This land is full of life. You just can't see it. Nor can I, nor Rosi, " he pointed down, "but Blanca and Gabriel can. Crazy Hawk too."

From the cockpit Marco gestured to the ground below. "You see, Hal, we're on our way to the Sonora Desert now, a place where plants can stuff themselves with enough water to last months of drought. Insects even devise their own refrigeration systems. And that sagebrush there," Marco nodded down to a plant that was so red it looked like it was on fire, "that survives any floods because it has a waxy jacket like a fisherman's coat."

Marco swerved the plane closer to the arid landscape below.

"I tell you both, it's here," He pointed down again. "Here, where the land has not been messed with yet." He wagged a finger at the two teenagers. "Here, where folks look out for each other instead of in at themselves. Right here, where nobody choses to live except a few Tarahumaras and old buzzards like Crazy Hawk." He smiled. "When all else has gone, I tell you, this is where life will hang on."

Hal and Rosalita took in Marco's words in silence, the plane now steady, its engine smooth.

"Well," said Rosalita, "I put it down to squirrel soup myself."

The three of them all burst into laughter, mostly out of the sheer relief of being alive.

Hal breathed in deep and thought about the last few days. Mexico had been way beyond the adventure his dad had promised him – and without a rare-breed butterfly in sight.

Hal realized he'd had a lot of firsts. He'd thrown his first punch, had his first plane ride, eaten his first cow lungs and his first squirrel, had his first contact with gangsters, been shot at for the first time and even, well sort of, celebrated his first kiss with Gina Moreno. And now he had another girl, a remarkable girl really, even if she was the rudest person he'd ever met, falling asleep on his lap…

*

"Hal! Wake up!" shouted Marco, turning and nudging Hal.

Marco turned back to the cockpit, flicking wildly at the instrument panel. The Skyhawk's engine was spluttering as if it had hiccups and a strange whirring noise, like a blender, came from inside the belly of the little aircraft.

Hal's nerves were once again on edge and Rosalita, still rubbing sleep from her eyes, had turned very pale.

"All OK, Marco?" Hal could scarcely hear himself speak amidst the throaty engine noises.

"Not sure," said Marco, "maybe one of those bullets Sol fired did do some damage after all. But don't panic, everything's probably fine. Nothing serious." Marco turned back and gave Hal an unconvincing smile.

"Marco!" Rosalita's voice was trying to sound calm but not succeeding. "What's that smoke coming out of the back of the plane." The engine hissed and groaned – it had gone from hiccups to full on whooping cough, the Skyhawk now rearing from side to side. Pancho had started to shake, slobber drooling from his mouth.

"Rosi! Hal!" said Marco, stabbing at the instrument panel again like a doctor on failing a life support system. "Buckle up and hold on tight. We're gonna have to land earlier than expected."

"By land," whispered Rosalita, squeezing the life out of Hal's hand, "I think he means crash."

Great, thought Hal, my first plane crash too. He held on to Rosalita's hand. Held it like he never wanted to let go.

Crash

Santiago stretched, lifted his face to the sun and let out a long, loud sigh. He knew nobody could hear him in this wilderness. Well, except maybe a sand grouse or a coyote.

After hitchhiking a thousand miles through Mexico, Santiago had jumped the border into America the previous night. Since then he had walked swiftly through the sand for almost twenty hours. He was beyond exhausted now, his eyes blood shot and droopy, his face dark from the relentless sun.

The determined migrant was proud he had now reached the USA. There were hardly any jobs in his village in the Mexican state of Chiapas, though he knew the situation was even worse for migrants further south from little countries like Nicaragua and Honduras. But Santiago was an optimist. He knew he could now find work in Arizona or California, maybe even Texas. Then he'd send some money home to his family. But he needed to stay alert all the time. If just one US border patrol saw him he'd be sent home pronto, all his efforts wasted.

Santiago ripped off his backpack and slumped down in the shadow of an ironwood tree. The tree was dead, struck by lightning in one of the many desert storms. Now it slumped dejectedly in the sand like a torpedoed ship.

This did not bother Santiago one bit. In this wilderness there weren't many big trees but the ironwood was a good size. It may have been dead but it still offered rare shelter from the fierce sun. Oh yes, shade! Precious shade! That was all Santiago cared about right now. It would give him somewhere to lie and sleep for a while, gather his thoughts.

Santiago snuggled into the cool sand beneath the ironwood. He smiled when he noticed a weed with bright blue flowers sprouting from the tree's bark. He ran his finger over the blue petals and remembered the time, years back, when his mother had told him: "weeds grow from nowhere, Santi, they are like the earth's dreams". His mom had never even been to school but Santiago always thought she was the smartest person he'd ever met. She had even learned English, partly by listening to songs by The Beatles, a British pop band, who many Mexicans loved. She, in turn, had taught her son the songs, and the language.

Before sleeping Santiago pulled out a photo of his faraway family – his wife, Rosa, and their toddler son, Polito. Holding the photo to his chest he softly began to sing, as his mother had taught him, first in Spanish, then English. It was always the same song. A much-loved Mexican ballad by the band *Los Jaguares de Juárez* – the Juárez Jaguars – about migrants far from home, about life on the road:

Ahí viene	Here he comes
caminando desde Oaxaca	Walking from Oaxaca
dejando su familia y su pueblo	Leaving his family, his home,
rumbo al otro lado,	En route to the other side,
a la frontera de los sueños y oportunidades.	The border of dreams.
Ahí viene,	Here he comes,
caminando por el desierto	A wanderer in the desert
con sus ahorros y con mucha sed,	Some pesos in his pocket
en busca de una nueva vida.	Full of thirst, free of spirit,
	Questing for a new life
Ahí viene	Here he comes
Ya llegó	Now he's already there
a la frontera	Near to the border
con el corazón lleno de esperanza	His heart filled with hope
pero con la barda y la migra encima...	But the fence awaits him...

Within a few minutes Santiago, mid-song, had fallen into a deep sleep. This blissful state lasted for several hours until he was roused by a strange noise, some kind of distant rumbling.

The migrant groaned and rolled out from under the tree, sand stuck to his face. He squinted towards the shimmering horizon. Something like a giant mosquito was heading straight for him, smoke belching from its tail. "*A bad dream*," he thought to himself. "*Must be.*"

He rubbed his eyes and squinted harder as the flying object hurtled closer towards him. Santiago was convinced, other than the stuttering engine noises, he could hear a dog howling. "Mother of God," he whispered, making an urgent sign of the cross on his chest. "What devil is *that*!"

Whatever it was, Santiago did not want to get in its way. It was now almost on top of him. He snatched his belongings and began to run…

*

The Skyhawk jiggered violently, shunting Hal and Rosalita towards the cockpit where Marco wrestled with the controls in a state of rising panic.

"Don't cut out on me now!" yelled Marco smashing his palm against the Skyhawk's windscreen. "Don't you dare!"

If Marco, normally the King of Cool, is acting like a headless chicken, thought Hal, then what chance have the rest of us got! Rosalita clearly thought the same, her breathing tense, her face frozen in terror.

"Come on, you heap of junk," shouted Marco, yanking at the joystick, "you can do this."

Rosalita was now grasping Hal as if he was a miracle branch –the only thing that would stop her tumbling through the sky. Pancho panted at her feet, letting out little yelps of fear, as Marco continued to curse in his fight to keep the engine alive.

It was a fight the veteran gangster was not going to win.

With one last rasp, the Skyhawk juddered, hissed and began its descent. Rosalita did not scream this time, all the passengers now stunned into deadly silence as they plummeted fast through the clouds, the only sound the Skyhawk's whirring propeller winding down and Pancho's now desperate howl.

The ground below them did not look like a promising airstrip, decided Hal, as he craned to look out. It was bleak stretch of hard sand studded with rocks, trees and huge cacti, many of them the height of football posts.

As the ground zoomed in towards them, Marco was battling with all his might to keep the Skyhawk level. The little plane was bucking about like a kite in a storm, a black, foul-smelling fan of smoke spewing from its tail.

"Hold on, amigos," yelled Marco, "this is it!"

The plane's propeller was still spinning with enough power to saw through the first obstacle, a giant cactus, its green, prickly flesh splatting over the cockpit glass. Seconds later the Skyhawk's wheels hit the ground. The plane bounced, out of control, and cleared the next cactus but its undercarriage scraped on a nearby boulder, sending up an angry shower of sparks.

Veering crazily from side to side the Cessna smashed directly into a mesquite tree, ripping off half its left wing. Before having any time to correct itself the second wing was severed by a boulder to its right. More sparks flew. Still the Skyhawk ploughed on, now looking more like a mini-subway train than an airplane.

And then the brakes finally took hold on the softening earth. A squat, chunky cactus brought the stricken Skyhawk to a halt, tipping it nose down, where it sat, like a giant insect burrowing into the sand, before slowly, creakily flipping over.

"Rosi! Hal!" Marco looked round urgently, his eyes wild, cheeks soaked in sweat. At the rear of the plane the teenagers were locked in an embrace that not even a welder could separate, Pancho licking at their faces.

"My God," whispered Rosi, looking up at Marco. "You did it. We're alive! We're ALIVE!" She smiled weakly. "Or is this heaven?"

"Being in my arms is heaven is it?" groaned Hal, wiping dust and sand from his face. He was badly shaken but was trying not to show it.

"Shut up, *cabroncito*." Rosalita punched him softly on the arm. "No way do I want the first person I meet up there to be a ginger freak."

"Well, amigos, that was our closest brush yet," said Marco, winking at them, "but I was always in complete control, of course!"

Pancho began to bark madly. Hal began to laugh, then Rosalita and finally Marco. All three of the Skyhawk survivors doubled up in hysterical, uncontrollable, 'can't believe we're still breathing' laughter.

"*¡Vámonos! ¡Vámonos! ¡Fuego! ¡Fuego!*" A voice shouted from outside, accompanied by fists banging. "Let's go! Let's go! Fire! Fire!"

The Skyhawk's door flew open, screeching horribly, instantly killing the laughter. A dark, stick thin man with panicked eyes pointed at the tail of the plane. "Fire! Fire!"

He held out his arm to Rosalita, who grabbed it without hesitation, and the grubby-faced stranger immediately pulled her out. Hal jumped out next with Pancho right behind. Marco still seemed dazed from the crash.

"*¡Vamos!*" the skinny man repeated, grabbing Marco's arm, "the plane is going to blow. Boom boom!"

Hal and Rosalita charged away from the smoldering wreckage, followed by Marco who was limping badly, propped up by their new friend and rescuer, who being a foot smaller than Marco, was using all his strength to drag the lumbering gangster through the sand.

"OK, OK, far enough," said the stranger, loosening his grip on Marco, who collapsed down against a mesquite tree. For a while all was quiet as the four of them stared at the plane, its tail now spewing up a long, fire-flecked trail of smoke. Within seconds the whole fuselage exploded. Hal felt Rosalita flinch next to him as bits of flaming debris landed in the sand in front of them.

Crazy Hawk Alabama won't be happy, thought Hal, as he watched the remains of the trusted Skyhawk explode a second time, sending up a final starburst of orange flames.

"Poor Skyhawk," Rosalita said, her bright eyes welled up with tears.

"Oh no..." whispered Hal, "when am I ever going to see my family?"

"You two!" shouted the stranger. "Help me. I think your dad's been knocked out."

"He's not our dad!" shouted Rosi, running over to Marco, while thinking to herself - but I wouldn't mind if he was.

The skinny man was wiping blood from Marco's temple. The old driver was slumped against the mesquite tree as if in a deep sleep.

"Sir, sir. Are you ok?" The good Samaritan gave Marco a sharp slap around the face. Nothing. "Sir, sir!" A harder slap. Marco groaned but his eyes stayed shut. The stranger drew his hand right back like a prizefighter and slapped Marco full in face.

The gangster's eyes sprung open. His expression was one of bewilderment, then fury. "Arrggh," he shouted, grabbing the stranger by the throat. "Who the hell are you, you devil?" The stranger reeled back, arms up in surrender, unable to speak.

"Stop it, Marco," yelled Hal, tugging at Marco's shoulders. "This man just saved our lives."

Marco threw off Hal with one hand and continued throttling the stranger with the other. "I said, who are you, you piece of dirt?"

"How can the poor man reply when you are strangling him," shouted Rosalita, pulling on Marco's shirt. "Let him free now! I order you!" Rosalita was shouting so loud she was turning red in the face. "Stop that now. I command you, Marco Rodríguez. Right NOW!" Rosalita fell backwards, she had pulled so hard on Marco's shirt part of its collar had ripped off.

Marco looked up at Rosalita in shock and then back at the stranger. "NOW! Right now! Please Marco," repeated Rosalita, softer this time. Reluctantly Marco eased his grip. The stranger dropped down on his knees in the sand, grasping at his throat. It took him some time to compose himself.

"My name is Santiago," the wounded man choked, pulling himself up from the ground. "I'm a truck driver from the south of Mexico. It's tough down there, no work." He rolled his eyes. "I jumped over the border into America so I can get a job, help my family. It's taken weeks. I've risked everything walking through this desert." He sighed and lifted his hands up. "Please, by the grace of God, don't hurt me."

"So you are a migrant worker," said Marco, his voice calm now, "and you say we're now in America?" Marco nodded in approval to himself. "If we are, I'm glad. We are safer here. I thought we were still in Mexico, south of the border."

"No, we are in America, sir," said Santiago. "We are in the Arizona desert and all I have are my clothes, a few snacks and a bottle of water."

Marco looked at Santiago for a long time, his eyes steady and unblinking. Oh no, thought Hal, please don't strangle the poor man again.

"I owe you a great apology, Santiago," said Marco, grabbing the stranger's forearm in a vice like grip. "Please forgive me." He smiled warmly. "You saved my life because I was too stupid, or too dazed, to jump from a burning airplane." Marco shook his head in shame. "All I did in return was try and kill you."

"I'm so sorry," the big man added, his knuckles turning white as his grip on Santiago's arm increased. "In my line of work I trust no-one. But you had no reason to trust us either and you risked your life saving us." He tightened his grip still more. "God bless you, Santiago. You are a true hero."

"Thank you, Sir," said Santiago, his face lighting up. He gestured to Marco's hand with his eyes. "Now can you please let go of my arm, I think it's about to fall off."

Marco smiled, released his grip and the tension between the two men fell away.

"So, I've told you who I am," said Santiago, "what about all of you?" He gave Pancho a pat on the head. "And this beautiful beast too?"

"Well, you've been honest with us," said Marco, his forehead creasing with a frown, "so we'd best be honest with you, amigo," His voice was uncharacteristically quiet and shy, as if confessing to a priest.

"I am Marco. I'm a Mexican gangster's pet thug, or at least I was." He gestured to Rosalita and Hal. "Rosi here is the gangster's daughter, and Hal is an English boy who was in the wrong place at the wrong time. Oh, and not forgetting Pancho, he's a Juárez street dog."

Santiago's jaw dropped. He looked so astonished he might as well have seen Pancho tap dancing.

"Don't worry, Santiago," chipped in Hal, attempting to lighten up the mood, "all Marco's said is true, but he's not a bad thug, he actually quite a nice thug really. Only kills people when he absolutely has to…" Marco gave Santiago his best gold tooth smile as if to confirm this.

"And Rosi here, well she's a bit crazy sometimes," Hal shrugged. "But she's pretty cool really and brave…"He cleared his throat. "Even if she is Tomas Ceto's daughter…"

"Tomas Ceto!" blurted out Santiago, making a sign of the cross on his chest. "You mean the most dangerous man in Mexico! You are his daughter, Rosi?"

"Well, sorry, yes," Rosi said, shrugging her shoulders. "That's my 'family'!"

"Mother of God!" said Santiago, shaking his head. "I should have left you all on the plane where you belong. Left you to fry." There was silence as the three Skyhawk survivors looked in disbelief at their new companion. Santiago sat downcast, his hands over his face, as he muttered miserably: "What have I done? What have I done?"

"Santiago?" whispered Hal. "Are you ok? We won't hurt you, we promise."

"Ha! Whoo! Yeehaa!" Santiago jumped to his feet making a series of whooping noises, slapping Hal on the back. "I'm only joking, you fools. Of course I'd have still saved you. You are my friends. I am a man of God and you are human beings aren't you? Well, except Panchito of course." He kissed the top of the surprised dog's head. "I was just so happy you weren't the border patrol. They'd have sent me back to Mexico in handcuffs even if I had saved you."

"You are probably right, Santiago," said Marco, relieved that their new friend was still on side. "But won't the border patrol come now. Won't they have heard us crash?"

"It's possible but I doubt it," replied Santiago, picking a prickle off a cactus stump. "We are in the middle of the Organ Pipe Cactus National Monument Park in Arizona." He gestured to the bleak, beautiful surroundings. "I jumped the fence far from the nearest border town. We are very remote now but don't worry, I've got a map." He tapped his shirt pocket.

"Does anyone else hang out here except the border patrol guys? asked Marco.

"Only a few campers and birdwatchers, but I've been walking miles from the main road." Santiago grinned. "It's been so lonely, you can't imagine. I'm actually glad to see you guys – even if you are a bunch of criminals and school kids." He put his arm over Marco's shoulders. "Just sorry you had to crash a plane to meet me."

*

For all the thrill of surviving the crash it soon became clear to the stranded party that they were still in grave danger.

Between them, they had very little. Santiago was travelling only with a small backpack. Inside it were two liters of water, a packet of custard cream biscuits, two cans of Spam and some jalapeño peppers. Hal had a half liter of water he kept in a bottle tied to his belt, a packet of Extra Strong Mints and an apple. Marco fumbled in his Jeans and proudly pulled out three, half-scrunched cigarettes.

"I've got some strawberry and vanilla lip balm," added Rosalita, holding it up in triumph, "if we get really desperate."

To make matters worse Santiago realized his map must have fallen out of his shirt pocket while he was rescuing everyone from the burning Skyhawk. Their only means of navigating to the nearest water supply was now up in smoke.

"Anyway guys, by the grace of God, we have each other, hey," said Santiago. "That still counts for a lot. In fact, if you are a traveling migrant on your own in the world, it means everything."

"Quite right," said Rosalita, smiling at Santiago. "If we work as a team we can get through this."

"We are all exhausted," said Marco, yawning. "And it's getting dark, starting to cool down. " He nodded towards the sun sitting low on the horizon. "You must be tired too Santiago, walking all day and then having to save us clowns. Let's share out a bit of food and water, get some rest and then make a plan."

"How about a bonfire?" suggested Hal, excited. "It will keep us warm and we can heat the Spam up."

"Nice idea, Ginger," said Marco, pulling out his lighter from his Jeans. "I can light it." He tapped a finger on his forehead. "You see, us smokers are smart. We have our uses after all."

"Are you two crazy!" said Santiago, laughing. "You really are a couple of city boys, aren't you? Or are you still stunned from the crash? We have a bonfire right there, just need to add a few mesquite branches." He pointed at the smoldering Skyhawk, where Rosi was already warming her hands.

"In the name of the Father," said Santiago, as he helped Hal steer the still limping Marco towards the plane. "That Rosi's ahead of the game, smarter than you two put together. And you were right on the money, little brother…" He grinned at Hal. "Considering she's Tomas Ceto's daughter, she's truly one cool girl."

Jerusalem

The party of four and their dog all nestled down in the sand, warmed by the glowing ruins of the Skyhawk. Hal and Rosalita bundled up together to preserve heat, but Santiago made it clear that Marco was going to sleep alone. Fair enough, considering the last time Santiago had woken Marco, he had tried to throttle him. Around them the smell of sizzling Skyhawk blended with the sweet, resinous aroma of burning mesquite branches.

Darkness fell fast and the exhausted posse, using random articles of clothing as pillows, fell straight to sleep on the sand, not even Pancho's snores stirring them.

Hal was the first to wake the following day. The sun had started to peep above the skyline, which was lined with the silhouettes of the cacti. The prickly giants stood like strange, multi-limbed sentries guarding the pink horizon.

Hal walked away from the Skyhawk, its heat now fading. After a couple of minutes crunching through the sand he stopped and peed, his breath smoking in the cold air.

He was so dehydrated his pee only lasted a few seconds. Hal was worried it smelled so toxic it might kill the surrounding cacti. He remembered seeing a survival program about a man called Bear who had drunk his own urine. As Hal's urine was a strange luminous gold color he decided against it. It looked even worse than when his mum had cooked beetroot stew and his pee had turned bright purple.

Up ahead, Hal heard a voice breaking the silence. An English voice! He looked up and saw someone marching towards him, hefting a backpack. The stranger was a small chubby man in his early twenties, waving around a walking stick, as if conducting an invisible orchestra. He wore jam-jar glasses, a pair of long blue shorts and a red handkerchief tied around his head. He was also listening to his iPod, singing along to a song Hal had never heard.

"Bring me my bow of burning gold!" bellowed the stranger.
"Bring me my arrows of desire!
Bring me my spear, O clouds unfold
Bring me my chariot of fire!"

Rosalita appeared beside Hal, her hair sticking up in an early morning frizz. She watched in fascination as the singing man wove his stick around.

"Who is *that*? she asked, rubbing the sleep out of her eyes.

"No idea," replied Hal, shaking his head. "But he looks harmless enough. Even if he does sing worse than my dad."

"I will not cease from mental fight," sang on the walking stranger, waving his stick with increasing fury. *"Nor shall my sword sleep in my hand..."*

"Mother of God," said Santiago, who had now appeared beside them. "What is that noise? It woke me up."

"Whatever the hell it is..." Marco stood behind them, looking like thunder. "I'm going to shoot it."

"Do you have to kill everything that wakes you, Marco my friend?" asked Santiago.

"Shh, he's started again," said Rosalita.

"Till we have built Jerusalem," sang on the stranger, shattering the silence of the desert. *"In England's green and pleasant land...."* He continued waving his stick as if trying to swat a wasp. *"Dum Dum Dum Dum, De, Dum De De Duuuuuuuuuuum..."*

"Hello there!" shouted Hal, waving his hands in the air.

"Ah, oh, oh… my goodness, good heavens above…" stuttered the singer, stopping in his tracks and ripping off his headphones. "I had no idea you were all there, I'm dreadfully sorry."

"So you should be…" whispered Marco.

"No problem at all, amigo," butted in Santiago, holding out his hand in welcome. "What's your name?"

"George," said the stranger, shaking hands with each of the group. "George Chattaway-Biggs." He smiled and peeled off the handkerchief on his head, revealing a mop of long, sun-bleached hair. "I love walking you see. Singing too."

"You call that singing…" muttered Marco, before Rosalita kicked him quiet.

"Oh, yes, I love singing," said George. "Good for the soul and all that. I was singing along to the hymn *Jerusalem*. I'm not a bible basher or anything but it's very stirring stuff, hey!"

"Er, I'm more of a heavy rock fan," said Hal. "AC/DC, The Killers, that sort of thing. But why are you walking in the middle of the desert, anyway? Your singing isn't that bad…"

"Oh, I see, yes," spluttered George. "Well, I'm on a long walk. A thousand miles actually." He gestured to the horizon with his stick. "From El Paso in Texas to San Diego in California. I love walking in remote places, the more remote the better…"

"It's ok, amigo, no need to be nervous," said Santiago, smiling at George. "Slow down."

"Yes, of course, sorry… sorry," George cleared his throat. "I'm a student you see. Just finished my degree in Spanish and Zoology at Oxford University." He took off his round glasses and began wiping them. "But more than anything I'm a twitcher."

"Twitter?" asked Marco.

"Titcher?" suggested Santiago.

"Twitcher," said Hal. "Means birdwatcher. My dad's one too."

"Yes, yes, I love my birds." George fluttered his hands as if to demonstrate. "I'm hoping to see many of our feathered friends here in the desert, especially the Costa's Hummingbird. Maybe even the Ruby-throated Hummingbird!" George fluttered his hands even faster. "Lovely little things hummingbirds, seventy wing beats a second and over a thousand heart beats a minute. Incredible hey." He gently pumped his chest to demonstrate. "And they only weigh about the same as a pound coin…"

"I don't understand a word this fool is saying," whispered Marco, in his thick Spanish. "He sounds like someone shoved a melon up his ass."

"Sshhh," hissed Rosalita.

"What about all of you?" asked George, his face pink, sweaty, eager. "Are you all looking for hummingbirds too?"

"Only if we can eat them," growled Marco, before Rosalita kicked him so hard he almost fell over.

"Have you got a phone, George?" asked Hal. "I really need to call home. My parents will be worried sick".

"Sorry, no, old chap," said George. "I like to escape when I'm out here. No contact with the outside world." He smiled. "Absolute bliss." He squinted into the distance. "Gosh, what's that smoke over there." George pointed at the still smoldering Skyhawk.

"It's an airplane…" Santiago began, then stopped, and said. "It's a bonfire!"

There was a long pause as Hal, Santiago, Rosalita and Marco all looked at each other, unsure what to say.

"Come and sit by our bonfire, George," said Hal, finally. "I'm from England like you, but my story is not such a simple one."

Twenty minutes later, huddled around the dying heat of the Skyhawk, Hal had finished explaining his story and the even more complicated stories of Marco, Rosalita and Santiago. He spoke as honestly as possible to the bewildered George. Hal was very careful to use words that would cause their new friend the minimum amount of alarm.

"Oh dear me," said George, sounding alarmed out of his head. "Dear oh dear. Let me get this straight. Between you…." He gestured to the group with his stick. "You are running from the police, the army, the border authorities and a couple of horrid, psychotic drug lords, one who just happens to be Rosi's dad and both of them Marco's ex-bosses."

"Yes, very well put," said Hal, nodding at George. "That sums it all up pretty well."

"And presumably you just want to get back to your parents, Hal?" added George, his eyes full of concern.

"Well, yes, of course," said Hal. "But it's not just me who needs help, we are a team."

"You are a fellow Englishman, Hal," stated George grandly. "I will help you in any way I can. I will also help Rosi as she is clearly just a girl. And judging by her face, not very well." Rosalita shot George a killer stare. "But, I'm afraid that's all I can do."

The sunburned student raised a finger in the air, eyeing up Marco and Santiago like a referee about to hand out yellow cards. "But that's it… and I mean this, Hal," George shoved his stick in the sand. "I point blank refuse to help any gangsters and illegal migrants."

"Then I don't want your help anyway," snapped Hal, ready to hit George. "They are my friends!"

Hal pointed one by one at Marco, Santiago and Rosalita. "Marco and Santiago have both saved my life and without Rosalita here, I'd have been dead long ago." Hal kicked at the ground, tears welling in his eyes. "I told you our story, didn't I, George? I was totally honest when I could have easily lied. And you say you won't help my friends." Hal gave the birdwatcher a furious glare. "You call yourself a fellow Englishman, blah, blah, blah. What a joke. Why don't you just walk away. Go looking for the red-faced flamingo or whatever it's called. You have no idea what we've all been through together."

There was a pause, the only sound a light breeze kicking up swirls of dust around them. George sat with his head down, deep in thought. After a couple of minutes, he looked up sheepishly.

"It's the ruby-throated hummingbird actually, old chap," he said to Hal, "not red-faced flamingo."

George gently put his hand on Hal's shoulder. "Look Hal, you are quite right, I wasn't thinking straight. Your story was all just a bit much to take in. I now feel utterly ashamed of myself." George shook his head. "You are still so young and you have been 100 percent straight and decent with me. By all accounts you have also been through quite an ordeal."

George leant on his stick and pulled himself from the sand. "I apologize to you, Hal, I really do, and your friends, too." He thrust out his chin. "I, George Chattaway-Biggs, vow to help all of you however I can, whether thug, migrant, schoolboy or drug lord's princess."

George put his hand over his heart. "You have my word, gentlemen! And err, lady." He bowed at Rosalita. "And, er, Mexican street dog." He patted Pancho's head. "If you are Hal's pals you are my pals." George lifted his stick in the air, like a knight about to charge into battle, and shouted at the top of his voice: "All for one and one for all!"

"I should have shot him when I had the chance," hissed Marco, under his breath.

"He's clearly bananas," Hal whispered to Rosi, "but at least he's on our side."

Pancho's Song

For all the group's initial doubts about George, he turned out to be much more help than expected. In his hefty backpack he had three liters of water, a cooking stove, cans of corned beef, sardines, pineapple chunks, a stash of granola bars, a compass and most importantly, a map. He also had enough books about hummingbirds to supply a village library.

After feasting on George's supplies, the group prepared to head straight to Lukeville, the nearest border town. Using George's map and compass they worked out – taking into account Marco's limp – it would be a two day walk. Once there, Hal could go to the border police who would help reunite him with his parents. George would hire a car (despite Marco's 'generous offer' to steal one) and drive Marco, Rosalita and Santiago to wherever they wanted to go: no questions asked.

They set off before it got too hot, marching at a good pace. Santiago and George walked either side of Marco to help him along. They progressed steadily taking only short breaks for snacks, water and to seek some shade from the fierce sun.

At the halfway point Marco shared out his spare cigarettes with Santiago and the two of them puffed away happily in the shadow of a cactus while George scanned the horizon for hummingbirds. Pancho enjoyed himself rolling around in the sand and tearing after a desert hare.

An hour before sunset, exhausted by their walk, they all foraged around for some mesquite branches. Then they lit a bonfire, Marco proudly whipping out his lighter to get it going.

George had lent Hal and Rosalita his iPod and, and after it got dark, they shared the headphones while warming their hands by the flames.

"George," said Hal as he flicked through their new friend's music collection, "do you have anything apart from classical music and weird bird noises?"

"Um, sorry, not really," George shook his head. "Oh, but yes, now I think of it, I've got some marvelous whales singing." His eyes glazed over, joyfully at the thought of it. "Absolutely soul charging stuff, recorded somewhere deep in the Pacific – the sound cuts right through you."

Hal turned the iPod onto full speaker and the beautiful, eerie blast of whale song echoed into the night. Pancho growled at the unfamiliar noises suspiciously.

"Sounds like me after too many chili tacos," said Marco, laughing. "Forget whales, chilies are what cut right through me, George."

"Ah, you are a such a joker, Marco." George slapped the Mexican on his back.

"George, my friend," said Marco, suddenly serious. "You may speak like you've got a melon up your ass," he flashed George a grin, "but you are a real gent, the finest twitter I ever met!"

"Twitcher, Marco," corrected George, prodding the older man's arm. "And you Marco, may speak like you are gargling rocks and vinegar, but you are the finest gangster I ever met." He frowned. "The only one, actually, thank goodness. No offence and all that."

"None taken, señor…"

"What's that noise?" said Hal, tipping his head to one side.

In the distance, Santiago was standing by a cactus looking up at the stars. He was singing quietly in Spanish.

"Come and join us, Santiago," called out Rosalita, "we could do with your company. You sound like the best singer of us all."

"No, no, I'm fine guys," Santiago said, waving them away. "Just thinking of my family. The song is one my father always used to sing to us as kids."

"Please sing it to us," said Rosalita, beckoning him over, "otherwise it's just going to be hummingbirds and love sick whales all night."

"Yes, yes, please do," said George. "I'd love to hear it too."

"OK, OK!" Santiago walked over and sat with the others around the fire.

"But I warn you it is very emotional," said Santiago, winking. "It's called *Pancho's Song*."

"*That name again!*" thought Hal. "*Dad would approve – and so would Pancho Villa.*"

"It's about a boy, " continued Santiago, "a boy called Pancho, and his girlfriend, Fernanda, who live in a little Mexican town near the border with Guatemala. The two young lovers carve their names on a cactus and swear undying love to each other." Santiago drew a heart in the sand with his finger.

"Pancho is too poor to marry Fernanda," added Santiago, his voice slow and serious. "So he sacrifices everything to go to America to find work. He is joined by two friends from his town…Enrique, who is bitten by a rattlesnake and heads home early and Carlos, who is caught by the border police and deported back to Mexico… Pancho nearly dies of thirst and hunger after getting lost in the desert but finally makes it to America and finds a low paid job on a ranch."

Santiago stopped and frowned, his forehead etched in small lines.

"So what happens?" asked Rosalita, eager for more.

"Pancho returns home many years later," continued Santiago, stabbing the fire with a stick. "He's almost an old man now. He finds the cactus and sees his name but Fernanda's has vanished. Pancho is so broken-hearted he collapses and weeps."

Santiago looked up at the others, who were all hooked by his story. "It is a song about lost dreams," he said, sighing. "But so much more than that."

The others all stayed quiet looking into the flames of the bonfire, each in their own world.

"You know, it makes me a bit ashamed," said George breaking the silence, his voice thoughtful. "Here I am trouncing about in the desert with a backpack full of food and gadgets and bird books. And just for fun!" He shot a fond look at Santiago. "But you are walking alone with practically nothing. Risking everything to give your family a better life." George nodded his head. "That's admirable Santiago, it really is."

"Don't beat yourself up, George," said Santiago, winking. "God deals us the cards he chooses. You are lucky, sure, but I am blessed in so many ways too. And I sure sing a hell of a lot better than you!"

"Amen to that," said Marco.

"So come on, Santiago," chipped in Rosalita. "What about your song. Please sing it."

"OK, Rosi." Santiago blew her a kiss, "just for you."

Santiago closed his eyes and took a deep breath. Then he was off, his soulful voice soaring through the heavy, mesquite-scented night.

Hal could only understand a few of the words but he could tell Santiago was singing with all his heart, singing with fury and tenderness about doomed graffiti on a cactus, about Mexico, about his life, about all of them.

Hal forgot his blistered feet, his exhausted limbs, forgot where he was, lost himself in a song he'd never heard before and yet had somehow heard a thousand times. Santiago sang on and on, finishing in a high-pitched crescendo, his head thrown back.

Nobody clapped or cheered and this seemed just right. Each of them was lost in their own thoughts. All was quiet except the backing chorus of the night –the breeze in the cacti, a desert owl hooting far away.

Rosalita wept quietly. Hal took her hand. The only movement was some fireflies, fizzing off wildly in the darkness, like stars being born.

*

"Hallelujah – I just saw a white-tailed kite," shouted George the next morning, charging through the cacti to greet his drowsy friends. "It must be nesting nearby," he enthused, still dressed only in his boxer shorts. "You have no idea how exciting this is, I've seen dozens of red kites near Oxford, splendid creatures, so poetic in flight, but this one…."

"George! Listen to me! " Marco sat up, half-dazed, rubbing the sleep from his eyes. "I don't care if you've seen a flying coyote. I don't care if you've seen Pancho Villa having tea with The Queen of England." He shook his head. "Just shut up when I'm sleeping. You get it, sshhhhh…"

"But it's a white-tailed kite Marco…"

Marco cocked his revolver and pointed it at George.

"OK, I see, yes, sorry," said George, putting up his hands. "I'll pipe down…"

Santiago began to laugh. "You are so lovely in the mornings, Marco, such a joy to be around!" Marco groaned, put down his gun and fell back heavily on the sand.

An hour later the party were all set to leave, having eaten some corned beef and biscuits and rationed out the water supplies for the day. All except George who thought he had heard a rare flycatcher and had bounded off in search of it still dressed only in his boxers.

As they all braced themselves for the long walk ahead, Pancho let out a loud yelp. The noise came from the mesquite bushes behind the bonfire. Hal dashed over to see what was wrong and found Pancho madly licking at his right leg.

"What's up, boy," said Hal, inspecting the spot Pancho was licking.

Santiago, now at Hal's side, leaned over to take a look. "It's just ants or something," he said. "In the worst case it might be a scorpion or even a snake. Did you see what happened?"

"Not really," said Hal. "Just heard him yelp."

"Are there really scorpions here?" asked Rosalita, who was also now crouched down by their side.

"Sure there are," said Santiago. " That's why I shook my boots this morning. Check none of the little beasts had got in." He smiled at Rosalita. "Don't worry, Pancho doesn't seem too unhappy. If it was a scorpion he'd be howling in pain. Let him rest a bit and if he doesn't get any worse, we'll get going in a few minutes. We need to reach the main road this evening."

Hal stroked Pancho's ears and the loyal dog whimpered, a noise that sounded part pleasure, part pain.

"Sounds like he's singing," said Santiago, laughing. "Pancho's Song. A very different kind of Pancho's Song to my one!"

"What's he singing about?" asked Rosalita, smiling at Hal. "What's going on in that doggy mind of his?"

Hal thought about everything that Pancho had witnessed over the last days. The poor hound had seen a lot: horrible underground garages sticky with blood, gunfights, plane crashes. Pancho's really seen human beings at their worst, thought Hal. Seen them shout at each other, hit each other, strangle each other and even shoot at each other.

"Poor Pancho," said Hal, "he must think us humans are all nuts."

Rosalita laughed, leaned over and gave Hal a kiss on the cheek,

"Don't worry, *cabroncito*," she whispered, as she peeled away, "Panchito's going to be fine. I promise."

And I suppose, thought Hal, smiling as he watched Rosalita walk away, that

Pancho had seen them all help each other too: rely on each other, trust each other. And maybe, just maybe, if the faithful dog looked really hard, saw through all the shouting, the fighting – he might have seen a bit of human beauty too.

Showdown

"Hello Hal, it's been a while. I've missed you."

Hal looked up but couldn't see anyone, the voice sounded familiar though. He had been comforting Pancho for a few minutes now and the relaxed dog was half asleep.

"Is that you, Rosi?" Hal arched his neck towards the ruined Cessna. "Rosi?"

"You should really call her Mariposa, Ginger Boy." Sol appeared from behind a cactus, holding a knife at Rosalita's neck. "That's her proper name. The one given to her by her father."

Hal was in a state of shock seeing Sol again. He felt his body pulse with terror, his heart quicken. "Be cool," he told himself. "Don't let psycho girl see your fear."

"So how did you find us, Sol?" asked Hal, as casually as he could manage. "You took your time."

"There was no rush." Sol smiled coldly. "Thanks to the chip I put in your shoe we always kept track of you. " She raised her eyebrows at him. "I'm slick like that, Ginger Boy, stuck it in your heel at the church in Creel. It's tiny, so I knew you'd never find it." Sol shrugged her shoulders. "I couldn't only rely on the bug in Mariposa's necklace. The one she smashed, stupid girl."

Rosalita kicked back, but her sister held her in an iron grip. Sol inched the knife tighter to Rosalita's throat, choking any words she wanted to say.

Hal's mind was in turmoil. Where were the others?

"We traced you during your flight, of course," continued Sol, her eyes invisible behind reflector sunglasses. "The plane fell out of the sky so fast it was clear you had crashed. Pity it wasn't fatal." She sighed to herself. "Now that would have solved a lot of problems!"

Sol pushed her sunglasses to the top of her head with her spare hand and gave Hal a strange look. "But you have a nasty habit of surviving, Ginger Boy. You, Marco and Mariposa. So I just kept tracing you as you crossed the desert…knew you wouldn't go anywhere fast and –abracadabra, here I am!" She flashed her dark eyes. "I never have any problems bribing my way across the border you see."

Sol pursed her lips and blew a kiss at Hal. "Always easy for a beautiful girl like me." She paused. "But my poor little sis, with her face, now would be another matter…"

Hal rose to his feet in fury as Rosalita battled once more against her sister's grip.

"Stop struggling, it's pathetic," snapped Sol, pushing Rosalita against a cactus stump. Rosalita screamed in pain. Sol pushed her sister down into the sand, where she lay still.

Pancho growled, the hackles on his back rising. Sol pointed her knife at him.

"I'll skin you for breakfast, you stupid mutt," warned Sol. "No more Señorita Sympathy this time, Ginger Boy." She waved a finger at Hal. "No more Miss Nice Girl."

"Miss Nice Girl!" said Hal, unable to keep his cool. "Any nice genes fled your body long ago along, Sol." His voice hardened. "Replaced by Psycho, Trigger-Happy, Do-What-Ever-My-Crazy-Drug-Lord-Daddy-says Girl genes."

Sol flushed in anger. She pointed the knife away from Pancho and drew it back over her head as if to throw it at Hal. Hal ducked down, his hands over his face.

"Jefa!" shouted someone by the bonfire. "Boss!" Sol looked over, distracted, Hal and Pancho temporarily spared.

Hal turned and recognized one of the thugs in black uniform who had been with Sol in Creel. He had some bruises on his face where Marco had thumped him in the church but otherwise looked fit. He was also holding a machine gun. Marco and Santiago were both already gagged and bound by the bonfire, sitting in the sand tied back to back.

The thug gestured to Santiago. *"Este hombre es nuevo, jefa,"* he said to Sol. "This man's new, boss."

"So who is he, Hal?" asked Sol, pointing her knife back at him. "Do tell?"

"Santiago's a migrant worker," said Hal. "He's done you no harm. You might as well let him go, he's nothing to do with all this."

"How touching. I'm impressed by how quickly you make new friends, Hal." Sol gave Santiago a disgusted look. "Not the sort of trash I'd ever invite into my home. But each to their own..."

Sol's phone rang, the jolly tinkling ringtone at odds with the violent atmosphere. Keeping her eyes on Hal, she flicked it open and put it to her ear.

"Hi Papi, yes, we've found them all," said Sol, her voice sounding obedient, child-like. "I parked the vehicle a couple of miles away and we crept up on them. They are all filthy and exhausted. No way of escape now."

There was a pause as Tomas Ceto spoke.

"OK Papi, I understand exactly what you want," continued Sol, nodding. "Bring Rosalita back and kill the rest. No problem. Love you." She flipped down the phone.

"You deal with Marco and the migrant," Sol snapped at the black uniformed guard. "Hal and Mariposa are mine."

Hal could hear Marco and Santiago groaning against their gags but was unable to make out any words.

"I thought your Papi told you to not to harm Mariposa," said Hal, his guts churning. "How can you kill your own sister?"

"He changed his mind!" yelled Sol, waving her knife at the still motionless Rosalita, "and she's not my sister. She's my rival."

"What rival?" shouted back Hal. "Rosalita doesn't want anything you have! Can't you see that." He slapped his palm hard against his forehead. "She ran away from that life, Sol, it's all yours now. "

Hal paused to calm himself down. He opened his hands towards Sol in appeal. "Do you really want to be like your Papi, Sol? He's just ordered you to kill me, a 14 year-old-school kid. That's as bad as Pretty Boy. The Toad's not even got the guts to do it himself," Hal raised his eyebrows, his voice hardening again. "Gets his lapdog daughter to do it for him. You're a joke, Sol. I feel sorry for you."

Sol glowered at Hal, her grip on the knife handle tightening. She looked properly angry: eye-popping, unable to speak, kidneys-about-to-explode furious.

Hal knew he was taking a big risk, but he didn't have many options. He could also see that his words, for the first time ever, were having an impact on Sol, chipping away at her ice cool mask. He was playing for as much time as he could get.

Over by the bonfire Hal heard the guard in black cocking his machine gun. Marco and Santiago sat stoically awaiting their fate.

Behind them Hal could see something. Oh my God. Yes! It was George! The bird watcher was tip-toing towards the bonfire, doing his best to hide behind the many cacti. He was treading on the sand with great caution, as if parts of it were electrified.

Hal looked down, so as not to give George's presence away. He knew the twitcher was their last hope. "*Hurry up, George!*" Hal thought to himself. "*You are not spotting hummingbirds now, this is desperate, do something!*" As if hearing Hal's request George shot out from behind a cactus brandishing his walking stick.

He charged forward, hurling his walking stick like a spear, hitting the startled black-unformed guard in the chest. The chubby, bespectacled birdwatcher had been transformed into a warrior. He still only wore his underpants, his blond hair sticking up like a punk and his mouth still dripping grease from his corned beef breakfast. He looked terrifying.

"Yaaaaaa" screamed George as he dived on top of the winded guard, knocking the gun from his hand. The two men grappled in the sand, each trying to reach the weapon.

At the same instant, Hal heard a scream as Rosalita, who had clearly been pretending to be hurt, grabbed Sol around her legs and wrestled her to the ground. Once Sol had fallen, Pancho bit into her hand and the knife fell. Hal grabbed it as the two sisters battled, Rosalita temporarily gaining control.

Taking advantage of Sol being disarmed, Hal charged over to Marco and Santiago, cut free their ropes and moved on to George. The bird watcher was in trouble, his head stuck in a brutal lock by the guard, who clearly now had the upper hand.

Hal picked up the guard's machine gun and held it to his shoulder. "Stop now or I'll shoot," he yelled. The guard didn't even look up and continued squeezing George's head. The student's face had turned a worrying shade of purple.

"Are you deaf?" shouted Hal, clutching the weapon awkwardly. "I said I'll shoot and I *will* shoot."

Still the guard did not release his grip, George now fighting to breathe.

"OK, that's it then!" said Hal.

"Hal don't shoot," warned Marco. "Give the gun to me."

But it was too late. Hal pointed the machine gun in the air and pulled the trigger, aiming to scare the guard and Sol into submission. He was immediately blasted backwards, shooting bullets everywhere, peppering the tops of cacti and the mesquites until he tripped over Pancho, falling on his back in the sand, the last bullets firing off towards the sun.

175

When he looked up, Pancho was licking at his face. Marco had overcome the guard, freeing George, and Santiago had helped Rosalita control Sol, who was still furiously straining against her sister's grip.

George pulled himself up from the ground clutching his throat.

"Good shooting," George smiled weakly at Hal, "I just hope you didn't hit any red-faced flamingoes."

Hal offered his water bottle to George while Marco tied up the guard. Sol finally stopped screaming insults and lay spread-eagled in the sand, Rosalita pining down her legs and Santiago her arms.

After the madness of the last minutes, a sense of calm returned.

*

The sound of a vehicle thrummed in the distance. "*What now*", thought Hal, standing up to see what fate would throw at them next.

The vehicle was a green and white Land Cruiser with the words **BORDER PATROL** written along its side. Hal breathed a sigh of relief. OK, so it might create a difficult situation for some of the party, especially Santiago, but it was better than being shot at by more of Tomas Ceto's goons.

The vehicle was travelling fast, kicking up a trail of dust as it chicaned through the boulders and cacti. It blazed towards them before skidding to a halt in front of the near dead bonfire. Out jumped three men from the back of the vehicle all in green border patrol uniforms –one of them wearing a red beret which was odd for a border patrol agent. All of them were armed with pistols.

"¡*Manos arriba!*" shouted Red Beret. "Hands up!" All the group slowly raised their hands, except Sol, who glared at them with hatred. "*Arriba!*" repeated Red Beret, pointing a gun at Sol's chest "Up!" She spat at him and begrudgingly raised her hands.

The Land Cruiser's driver door flung open and out stepped Pretty Boy. He was wearing a leather jacket and blue Jeans, his hair, as usual, shiny with grease. A small, black hand-grenade was clipped to his belt. Seconds after Javier leapt from the passenger door, sporting exactly the same clothes and hairstyle as his father.

Pretty Boy paced up to his new prisoners. Thanks to Marco's surgery in the cave, Pretty Boy now had a scar shaped liked a butterfly's wings on his forehead, making him look like a tribal chief. This was not a look that the vain, baby-faced gangster liked at all but he wasn't going to admit it.

"Hello, Marco, old friend," said Pretty Boy, grinning, his teeth the usual neon white, except one in the middle which was missing. You did a good job, Marco, thought Hal, the missing tooth makes Pretty Boy look like a village idiot.

"So, here we are again," said Pretty Boy. He now stood directly in front of Marco, the two enemies eye to eye. "I suppose you gave me a butterfly scar to remind me of your beloved Mariposa, didn't you?" He sighed. "Remind me that I wounded her. Not that it bothers me much. I'd happily shoot any of Tomas Ceto's family." He pointed at Sol. "Her too."

Javier laughed. He stood next to Hal, pointing a gun in his back.

"Don't worry, you worm," Javier whispered in Hal's ear, "you won't be left out when the shooting starts." He cast a look at Pancho, who was sitting at Hal's feet. "And we'll kill the mutt this time. He's too soft for dog fights anyway."

"Shut up, Javier," snapped his father. "We have work to do."

"Yes, Papi, sorry," said Javier.

"Yes, Papi, sorry," echoed Hal under his breath, rolling his eyes at Javier in disgust.

Pretty Boy looked around at the assembled party and settled his eyes on Mariposa. He walked over to her.

"So lovely to see you, Little Butterfly," purred Pretty Boy, stroking her cheek.

"How did you find us?" Rosalita asked, her voice shaking with a mixture of fear and rage. "How did you get the American patrol vehicle?"

"We hijacked it, my dear," said Pretty Boy. "The gringos patrol very close to the border and sometimes cross. My men held the driver and passenger at gunpoint and they flashed their passes as we crossed the border into America. Clever hey?" Pretty Boy winked at Mariposa. "Once in the desert we forced the three captured men to radio back and tell their boss all was fine. My men tied them up to a cactus and put on their uniforms. Piece of cake!" Pretty Boy shrugged his shoulders. "But even so, my dear, time is pressing, they will find out sooner or later."

"But how did you track us here in the desert?" asked Hal, playing for more time. "We are in the middle of nowhere."

"Ah, young Hal, still with us I see," said Pretty Boy, sneering. "Quite the survivor, aren't we." He flashed Hal a chilly glance. "We knew where you were because we tagged Marco. He has a watch he never takes off, given to him by his darling Rosi, I believe. Big, chunky cheap thing, so easy to put a chip in. Been bugging him ever since he worked for me. Never really trusted him from the start."

Pretty Boy's eyes narrowed at Marco. "We've been watching you all for some time but wanted to wait until Sol was with you and...what's that beautiful saying – kill two birds with one stone. We never had a chance in Creel. Too public for us, but out here...perfect!"

"My father will kill you for this, Pretty Boy," shouted Sol, "and your son!"

"Yeah right," said Javier, taunting her. "An old, washed up toad. How very scary! He's nothing without you, Sol, and you know it." He grinned. "But I like your style, beautiful, you are quite a girl. We could spare you if you join us..."

Sol screamed and spat towards Javier.

"Oh well," said Javier, shrugging, "you had your chance."

"And now, my dears, no more time to chat," Pretty Boy held up his pistol and gave it an admiring look, "after all, we have so many people to deal with. Now, where shall we start!"

Pretty Boy wandered around his prisoners.

"What can we do", thought Hal, *"the situation is impossible!"* All five of them were exhausted, two of them were teenagers, one a half-strangled birdwatcher and the other two both tough guys but unarmed. Sol's thug was still bound up and with Sol it was impossible to know who she would fight for. Pretty Boy's team was all armed, unwounded and had no scruples about who they killed.

"Maybe we should start with Mariposa," said Pretty Boy, walking up behind Rosalita. "Finish the job I started five years ago. After all Marco has knocked out one of my teeth and carved a butterfly scar on me." Pretty Boy ran his hand across his forehead, outlining the wound. "A way for me to remember what I did."

Pretty Boy turned to Marco. "But when there's time I have surgeons who will heal my scars, dentists who will cure my teeth, but you have no-one who can do anything for you, Marco, do you?" He gave his enemy a tight smile. "I will kill you too, old friend, of course I will. But why not snuff out your Little Butterfly first. Give you a nice mental scar before it's your turn."

"Pretty Boy," whispered Marco, his eyes hard and still, "you truly are a monster."

"Perhaps," said Pretty Boy, "but you have done things just as bad as me. You say you have changed, but have you really?" Pretty Boy clicked his fingers. "Anyway, amigo, let's not get bogged down in detail. The next question is who will deal with Mariposa?"

"What do you mean?" asked Marco, horrified.

"Well, I might ask Sol to do it," said Pretty Boy, grinning. "She hates her sister even more than I do. She thinks Mariposa told the police where her dad was hiding after the Mexico City shooting five years ago. Thinks the Little Butterfly gave away her Papi's jungle hideaway after she fled to the Pastor's place with you." Pretty Boy shook his head. "Thinks she's a dirty traitor."

"But it was Mariposa!" shouted Sol, straining against the grip of Red Beret. "It had to be!"

"No it wasn't, Sol darling," said Pretty Boy, laughing cruelly. "It was me actually." He paused and flicked back his hair. " You see, Luis Ramírez, the policeman who arrested your father in the jungle was corrupt. He was working for me, not the government. I paid him a huge amount to put all the police resources into finding Tomas Ceto." Pretty Boy grinned. "He didn't let me down and focused only on your dad until he tracked him. Poor cop, he's still being held prisoner..." Pretty Boy winked at Sol. "I believe you might know something about that..."

"You idiot, Sol," shouted Mariposa. "I hate Papi, but I'm no traitor. How could you have believed I would give him up? Or give up you?"

Sol looked at the ground in shame, her thoughts in a tailspin. "I'm sorry, Mariposa," she said softly. "I made a big mistake."

"Oh, dear," said Pretty Boy, enjoying his sense of power. "You sisters can have a hug later. Oh sorry, no you can't," he clicked his fingers, laughing. "Because you will both be dead."

"You are sick in the head, Pretty Boy," said Marco. "What happened to you to make you so messed up?"

"Oh, call the brain doctors shall we, Marco," said Pretty Boy, smirking and clicking his fingers. "Bring in the shrinks, the men in white coats. Strap me up in a straight jacket." Pretty Boy clapped his hands. "Ha! Please, old friend, I'm perfectly fine. I'm just protecting my family business, like a good son should. Doing what my father did."

"I'm glad I never met your father," whispered Hal.

"Alright enough!" shouted Pretty Boy. "If Sol isn't going to shoot Mariposa, who will?"

Pretty Boy put his finger to his lips. "Mmmm, let me see. Marco never would, nor Hal, and I've no idea who Blondie over here is." He pointed at George. "Or this little man." Santiago gave him a cold stare.

Pretty Boy tapped his head as if having a sudden brainwave.

"I know exactly who will do the honors," said Pretty Boy. He turned to Javier, handing him his pistol. "Son, it is time for you to draw first blood. You are about the same age I was. I know you are keen to kill Hal, and that can come later. But let's start with the Little Butterfly."

Javier took the pistol from his father as if it was the most precious thing he'd ever seen.

"Thank you, Papi." Javier cooed and walked over to Rosalita. "Blindfold her," he shouted at Red Beret.

"I don't want a blindfold," yelled Rosalita, wrestling with Red Beret as he applied a strip of dark cotton around her eyes. "Are you afraid to look me in the eyes when you shoot me, Javier? You little coward."

Despite Rosalita putting up a valiant fight Red Beret soon had the blindfold on. Hal looked in horror, desperately thinking how to save his friend. As he had a gun pointed in his back, his options were limited.

"Put her over here," ordered Pretty Boy. Red Beret dragged the screaming Rosalita in front of a cactus near to where Marco stood.

"I want you to see this Marco," said Pretty Boy. "Front row seats!"

Marco stood silent and helpless, a furious look on his face.

"Do it, Javier," said Pretty Boy, clicking his fingers. "Do it now!"

Javier raised the pistol. This was a moment he had been dreaming about, his chance to make his father proud. Javier spread his feet and took aim at Mariposa's chest. At first his hands stayed still as a surgeon, but then began to shake a little. He took a deep breath to steady himself.

"You don't have to do this, Javier," shouted Hal. "You are about to shoot a girl in a blindfold, you are better than that." Red Beret grabbed Hal. "You are better than your father…"Hal was silenced a guard's hand over his mouth..

Javier shot a look at Hal and dropped the gun slightly.

"Do it, Javier!" snapped Pretty Boy, his anger increasing at his son's hesitation.

Javier lifted the gun again, jolted by his father's words. In front of him Rosalita had begun to weep quietly.

"Please Javier," she said, putting her hands together in prayer.

"Don't do this, Javier," hissed Marco. "Talking of killing and actually killing are two different things. You can have a better life, different to your father…be brave, put down the gun…"

Red Beret held his pistol under Marco's nose, silencing him.

All was quiet except the breeze rippling the sand. Javier walked another pace towards Rosalita and held up the gun once again. This time his hands were shaking uncontrollably, as if he was stricken with some fatal disease. He kept desperately trying to steady himself, to muster some strength from deep within him, but he was beyond help: broken.

"I can't Papi," Javier whispered, lowering his gun in shame, "please, I just can't do it."

Pretty Boy walked over, a look of disdain on his usually unflappable face.

"You are not worthy to be my son." His voice was quiet but full of bitterness. "Give me the gun, Javier. Give it to me right now."

Javier handed over the weapon miserably, like a child letting go of a confiscated toy. Pretty Boy took the gun. He held its short barrel up to his nose and sniffed as if inhaling the scent of some exquisite flower.

"Oh well," Pretty Boy smiled at Marco, "sometimes you just have to do the job yourself."

Pretty Boy raised the gun fast, hands still and firm, aiming directly at Mariposa. "Goodbye, Little Butterfly."

Fzzt!

Sol hurled herself at Pretty Boy just before the shot rang out. She propelled herself directly in the line of fire, shielding Mariposa from harm. The bullet hit her hard in the chest sending her flying into Mariposa.

Mariposa screamed, feeling the weight of her sister against her, but still blind as to what had happened. Marco ran over, ripping the blindfold off Rosalita as he knelt down to cradle Sol in his arms. The Sun Queen was limp, her breathing shallow.

Rosalita looked down at her wounded sister. She leaned over Sol's face, mute with shock, unable to believe what she was seeing: her once invincible elder sister, usually so strong, so full of pride, now lying broken and weak, a soft, unfamiliar look on her face.

"Mariposa." Sol's eyes welled with tears. She reached out weakly and stroked her little sister's cheek. "Forgive me." She gave her sister a brief smile, her bright eyes no longer hard but full of affection. "You were always the best of us."

"No, Sol, no," Rosalita whispered, clasping her sister's hand, "you will be ok. You have to be. Sol... Sol, please, Sol..."

Sol shifted her gaze to Marco, her eyes soft, her look tender. She strained her face towards the old driver as he put his ear down to hear her.

"Save Mariposa." Sol's voice was urgent, but no more than a whisper. "Save her, dear friend."

Sol's breath gave out, her head slumped back as Marco gently kissed her forehead. Rosalita thumped at the sand with her fists, sobbing uncontrollably. Hal moved forward to comfort her but was pushed back by Red Beret. George and Santiago watched on, unable to act, both hemmed in by the other armed guards.

"What a touching sight," said Pretty Boy, standing over Sol, gun by his side. "All a bit unexpected, I have to admit. Upset the timetable, but no skin off my nose." He shrugged, grinning. "So let's see. Where were we now? That's it. One of Tomas Ceto's daughter's down." Pretty Boy drew a one in the air with his finger. "One to go!"

Marco looked up, his eyes calm and unblinking. "I don't think so, Pretty Boy. Not this time."

Marco launched himself up with tremendous force scooping Pretty Boy off his feet. He surged forward like a one-man juggernaut sending the drug lord scrunching hard against the nearest cactus. Pretty Boy screamed in pain as the cactus's spikes skewered into him.

Marco clutched his opponent in a deadly embrace, his own arms bleeding freely, but the old driver was now in a state beyond pain, his adrenaline off the scale, his focus unwavering.

Marco reached down and pulled out the hand-grenade Pretty Boy had clipped to his belt. "Stand back," he shouted at the surrounding guards, holding the grenade in the air for them all to see, "one move and I pull the pin."

"So, just you and me, amigo." Marco looked hard into Pretty Boy's terrified eyes. "Not such a tough guy now, are you?" Marco held the grenade in Pretty Boy's face. "Not even the best surgeon in the world will heal this, you coward."

"Don't Marco," begged Pretty Boy, sick with fear, "you will kill us both."

"Yes I will," whispered Marco, he twisted his neck around to face the others.

"Hal! Santiago! George! It's been an honor, gentlemen," Marco shouted out. "Tell Crazy Hawk he's my best friend in the world and that I'm sorry about his Skyhawk." The old gangster turned his head another notch, paused, and smiled at Rosalita. "And you, my brave girl," Marco's voice cracked but remained clear, "if ever I had a child, Rosi, trust me, I'd want her to be just like you." He winked. "Wouldn't change a hair on your beautiful head."

Marco ripped out the grenade pin with his teeth and dropped it down Pretty Boy's shirt.

"For you, Sol," he said.

Marco held Pretty Boy up against the cactus in his fierce embrace as, whimpering with terror, the drug lord struggled frantically to escape.

A muted explosion ripped across the desert, as Pretty Boy shot upwards, his body landing on one of the giant cactus limbs, his complexion punctured with dozens of little spikes. Marco collapsed head down in the sand below him.

Hal watched in horror unable to move. He knew he had to act if he was to survive, but his body was in a state of shock - frozen. He looked across at Marco's body with Rosalita crying over it.

Red Beret had his back turned to Hal. He was being distracted by Javier who was standing in front of Rosalita. It looked like Javier was trying to defend her from the thuggish commando, who was waving his gun at her. Hal knew he must defend Rosalita at all costs. A fierce anger sparked inside him. He took a deep breath and braced himself to attack Red Beret.

Shots began firing all over the place. Hal saw Red Beret clutch his arm, then there was a loud explosion, Hal felt his legs fall from under him, his vision going. He could hear George asking: "Hal, are you ok, old chap?" and saw Santiago's concerned face above him…and then Rosalita was there… yes, Rosi was there, holding his hand in that finger-breaking way of hers… and then… Who was that?… It was a face he knew but Hal couldn't place it… oh that's it, it was Mr B… good old Mr B, his neighbor, cider guts, Craddly Hill…what on earth was he doing here?…and then he pictured his mum and dad and Abby… then he felt Pancho lick his cheek… and then a blur of noise and swirling dark shapes….and then he was lost…pulled in a vortex…gone.

PART FOUR

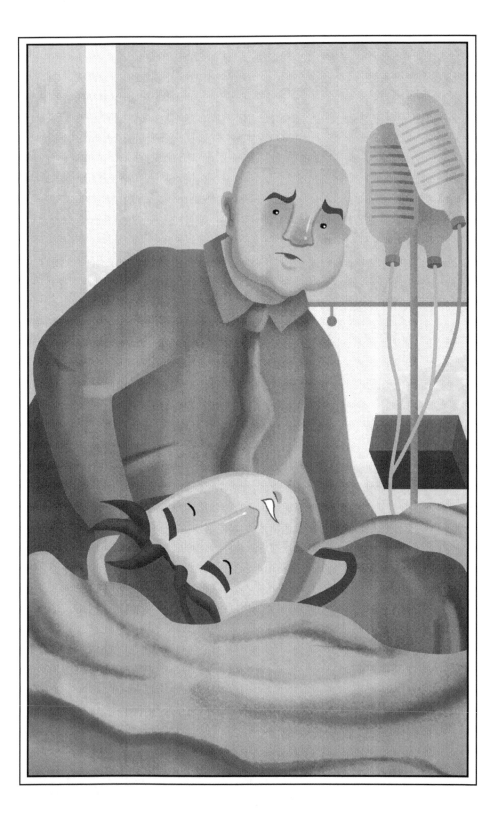

The Black Unicorn

Hal woke and sat upright with a jolt. He saw his reflection in a mirror opposite his bed. His face was pale and sweaty as old cheese, his eyes puffy, a bandage wrapped around his forehead. His body felt cold and stiff. Ouch, he thought, staring at the mirror, is that pale, lank-haired dork really me?

Glancing at some flowers on his bedside table, Hal realized he was in a hospital. There were a few cards and a half deflated balloon stuck to the ceiling. The curtains were shut and other than a drip connected to his arm making soft, regular beeping noises, all was quiet. It must be night, thought Hal.

The door opened and in came Mr B with a young, smart-uniformed nurse.

"Hey honey," said the nurse in a laid back southern Californian accent, "good to have you back in the land of the living."

"Thank God, Halford," said Mr B, sitting down at the bedside. He clutched Hal's shoulder as the nurse checked his drip. "We've been waiting for over a day."

Hal looked his elderly neighbor up and down. "I don't want to be rude or anything, Mr B," Hal paused, "but, I mean…just what are you doing here?" Hal stopped again, gathering his thoughts. "Where's Rosi?... And Santiago and George?... I remember Sol and Marco are…gone." He frowned, his eyes welling up. The nurse noticed Hal's discomfort and quietly left the room. "And what happened to me?" added Hal, wiping tears from his eyes. "I feel so weak."

"Rosi's fine, Halford, so are Santiago and George," said Mr B softly. "Terrible about poor Marco and Sol but one thing at a time, hey." He gestured to Hal's bandage. "You'll be fine too but you've been through hell and back, old son. Handled yourself like a trooper…"

"Why am I here?" Hal interrupted. "Why are nurses fussing over me?"

"You were grazed on your forehead by a bullet. If you remember, there was a shootout in the desert…"

"Grazed by a bullet in a shootout!" Hal smiled weakly. "That actually sounds pretty cool."

"Well, if you say so," said Mr B, frowning. "It was a rubber bullet, you see, but still gave you a nasty nick." Mr B shook his head. "Ricocheted off a damned boulder."

"Who fired it?" asked Hal.

"It was me, actually. Terribly sorry, old son. An accident…"

"You!" said Hal, gob smacked. "You shot me? What were *you* doing there? You live in Craddly Hill!"

"Well, yes, I do sometimes," said Mr B, choosing his words carefully, "but after I retired from the navy I did a lot of undercover work for the American DEA… that's the Drug Enforcement Agency." He smiled. "They first approached me when a couple of Mexican drug lords showed up in London. The DEA were impressed by my spy work so posted me to the Tex-Mex border - the heart of the drug war. I know I sound very English but I'm actually half American, born in San Diego in California, where we are now. Means I speak Spanish like a Mexican." Mr B waved his hand in the air with a flourish. "*Sí, sí, Señor Halford.*"

Hal looked at the ex-naval officer in disbelief as if he had just performed a triple somersault.

"I thought your only skill was walking Pancho," said Hal, grinning, "and you weren't very good at that. You really are a dark horse, aren't you, Mr B?"

"Well, put it like this," replied Hal's neighbor, a hint of pride in his voice, "my colleagues don't nickname me The Black Unicorn for nothing." He tapped his nose. "The people who appear the most ordinary are the best ones to surprise you."

"So tell me more, Black Unicorn," said Hal, "there's still a lot I don't understand."

Mr B explained that Johnny Bradby had phoned him in Craddly Hill as soon as Hal and Rosi had been kidnapped at the Pastor's place. Hal's dad was one of the few people who knew Mr B was still a highly trained undercover agent.

"After your dad's call I was in touch with my old DEA friends quick as a flash," explained Mr B. "They shut down any newspaper stories about you in Mexico and America pronto. If your name had appeared on the news, Hal, you might be on the drug cartels' hit lists forever. Both Pretty Boy's and *El Sapo's* men would be out for your blood."

"So nobody knows I'm here?" asked Hal.

"Only me, your parents, a few DEA agents and Rosi, Santiago and George," said Mr B, tapping his nose again. "We need to make it look as if nothing unusual has happened to you…that you just spent a bit longer at The Pastor's place than expected"

"Fair enough, I suppose," said Hal. He suddenly grabbed Mr B's wrist. "But what about Rosi? Please tell me. She must be in danger too. Can I see her?"

"Absolutely not," replied Mr B. "She's safe but it's too much of a risk to tell you where she is. We must let things calm down a bit."

"And Mum and Dad?" pleaded Hal. "Abby?"

"They're fine but it's still too risky," stressed Mr B, his voice soft and patient. "This is a very secret location but we can never be too sure. Pretty Boy is dead, Sol is dead and so is Marco. All the drug gangs will be thirsty for revenge. It will cool down, but it may all heat up too." Mr B smiled at Hal fondly. "Besides you need some time to recover. A few weeks."

"But surely I can at least speak to them?" asked Hal, his voice beginning to sound drowsy.

"I repeat, Halford," stressed Mr B, "any live communication is strictly off limits." He shrugged his shoulders. "I'm sorry, old son, but you will speak to your family soon, I promise. For now I have some recorded messages from all of them." Mr B smiled, pulled a CD from his pocket and Frisbeed it onto Hal's lap. "You'll enjoy watching it. They can't wait to see you."

"Is there a message from Rosi?" asked Hal.

"Not yet," said Mr B, "you can meet her when the time is right, trust me on this."

"I suppose I'll have to," said Hal. "After all, you are The Black Unicorn."

"Too right I am," said Mr B. He handed the laptop to Hal.

"No wifi here, old son," warned Mr B. "But you can watch your family's messages as many times as you like." He raised himself from the bedside. "I'll let you have some privacy, but I'm here if you need me."

"Just one more thing." Hal raised his hand as if back at school. "You said you were the one who fired the bullet, Mr B," he shrugged, "so how did you find us?"

"Ah yes, of course," said The Black Unicorn, nodding. "Those three border agents Pretty Boy tied to a cactus were found by a party of American birdwatchers. Once freed, the agents phoned the DEA in El Paso, where I was based." Mr B ran a hand through his non-existent hair. "We had a bug on Pretty Boy and knew he would lead us to you, so we flew a helicopter over to scan the area…by the time we got to you there was already gunfire…we had to shoot from the chopper, a combination of tear gas and rubber bullets." Mr B looked through an imaginary rifle sight. "Bang! Bang! Bang! We took out all the men in uniforms from quite a distance. I'm still a handy marksman, believe it or not, and wounded the thug with the red beret." He shook his head. "One of my bullets pinged off a rock and hit you. We landed the chopper as fast as possible but I'm really sorry you had to get injured, old son."

"That's ok," said Hal, shifting up in his bed, "your shot probably saved Rosalita's life."

"Pretty Boy's lad deserves most of the credit for that," said Mr B. "Javier's his name isn't it? He was standing in front of Rosalita, protecting her from one of his father's henchmen. " Mr B shook his head. "Poor lad had just seen his dad blasted to smithereens too. He's being held in El Paso now. We're not sure what to do with him."

"Be fair," said Hal, sleepily. "He's a total fruitcake but he did have the childhood from hell."

"Ok, young Halford, you get some sleep," Mr B saluted at Hal as he headed for the door. "You deserve it."

"Will do, Black Unicorn, Sir," replied Hal, saluting back. He still had so many questions but he felt beyond exhausted now.

Hal yawned and fell back on his pillow. He opened the laptop, propped it on his lap and booted up the CD Mr B had given him, the little device whirring hard.

Hal's Mum, Dad, Abby and Pancho instantly appeared on screen. They were sitting in a row on the sofa at Craddly Hill and all talking at once.

"Come home soon, smelly bum!" shouted Abby.

"You are so grounded, Hal Bradby," warned his mum, blowing him kisses and crying her eyes out. "And your dad is too!"

"We never did see any butterflies did we?" said Johnny Bradby. "I'm so sorry what I put you through, son, and so proud of you. I'd do anything to be with you now, but Mr B has told us to keep away. Can't wait to see you, Hal. Mr B will keep you safe…" He winked and said in a hushed, comic voice. "Sorry, by Mr B, I actually mean, shhh…The Black Unicorn!"

In the background Pancho wagged his tail, holding a Union Jack cushion in his grinny mouth.

Hal reached out to touch the screen. Ten minutes later the nurse came back and found him asleep, hugging the laptop tight to his chest.

*

Over the next week Mr B visited Hal regularly, one time dropping off a letter for him. The Black Unicorn had insisted that written and recorded messages were the only way to communicate for now.

The letter was from George and penned in wild handwriting that swooped about like one of his beloved hummingbirds:

How's tricks, Hal?

I hope you are flying down the road to recovery swift as a peregrine falcon. If you didn't know, peregrine falcons are amazing, the fastest birds in the world, can dive over 200 miles an hour Oh, shut up George, I hear you say, enough birder talk!

You won't believe where I am Miracles in Hell! They all speak very fondly of you here, and of course, Rosi, and dear old Marco. I still shed tears about what Marco did that day. He was not only the finest gangster I ever met but also one of the very finest human beings. We put up a little cross in his honor here. I sang Jerusalem and imagined Marco waking up from the dead and thumping me!

But the main reason I came here, Hal, was to bring back Pancho. The Pastor and Jose were so pleased to see him. Rosi asked me to do this. She's in some secret location and I hope to God she's ok.

When we first met Hal, I said something so wrong about Rosi. Said I'd help her because "she was just a girl and probably ill because of her face", or something like that. Hal, I can't tell you what shame I feel about this now. Rosi is one of the most lovely, remarkable girls to ever walk this earth. I just say the daftest things sometimes. I hope you can forgive me.

I love it here at Miracles in Hell. The Pastor, Jose and the gang are all top bananas. After all that happened to us in the desert, I've decided to put my trip to good use rather than just spying 'red-headed flamingos' as you'd call them. I'm going to take Pancho on his longest walk ever 1000 miles from here to Tijuana! Any money people give Pancho and I for our efforts will go to Miracles in Hell. Good idea, hey? And I will do it all in memory of Marco.

So that's my news. I only wish Santiago's story had a happier ending. I'm sure you know he's now in a detention center on the border, soon to be sent home. I gave him all the cash I could spare but I'm just a student so it wasn't much. He deals with his fate with such grace, an example to us all. I will never forget that song he sang around the campfire. I doubt he'll forget the loved up whales either!

All good wishes, Hal, and do stay in touch.

All for one and one for all!

George

A few days after reading this Hal woke up one morning to find another letter on his bedside table. On the envelope in very small, immaculate writing were the words: "Hal Bradby". Hal ripped it apart and read…

Hola Hal,

I expect you thought this was from Mariposa and thrilled to receive it. I'm sorry to disappoint you, Ginger Boy, but it's from me, the other Ceto sibling –Psycho Girl, The Ugly Sister, The Bad Seed. That's right, it's Sol.

I'm too much of a coward to see you face to face so I slipped in disguised as a nurse and dropped the letter off while you were sleeping. I've always been a sneaky little rat. I've been recovering in the same secret hospital as you, but Mr B wanted everyone, including Mariposa, to think I'm dead. That way, the papers will think I'm dead too. Mr B has done well keeping my sister and me out of the news.

So, you probably hoped I was dead, Ginger Boy. In some ways I did myself. I'm so ashamed of myself: my jealousy, my cruelty, my complete devotion to my father, a man who would happily kill his own children.

That terrible day when Marco died, seeing Javier's blind obedience to Pretty Boy, made me realize what a pathetic fool I'd been obeying The Toad all these years. Then hearing that it was Pretty Boy, not Mariposa, who blew Papi's cover all those years ago, my insides collapsed. I wasn't human anymore, just a hollow shell, my guts ripped out.

 That's why I jumped in front of Pretty Boy's bullet. I wanted to save Mariposa but I also no longer cared if I lived or died. I'd almost forgotten that I had a bulletproof vest on. Papi always insisted on it, his one bit of useful advice. The shot was fired so close it crushed my ribs and lungs and bruised the hell out of me, but for better or worse, I'll live.

And I want to live now, Ginger Boy. I want to do everything in my power to support and protect my little sister. I can't even bear to think what that poor girl has gone through. She stood up to the most violent men in Mexico: tiny, delicate, bold as a jaguar Mariposa. For all my jealousy, she is, was, and always will be, my heroine. If I can ever show just a tiny bit of her courage, I will die happy.

So, why am I writing to you, Ginger Boy, someone I'd have happily shot a few days ago without a second thought. Well, for starters, I want to thank you for being a friend to my sister. I also want to see her again and I want you to be there too. In truth, I'm terrified of meeting her on my own. She may choose to hit me, run from me or kiss me, who knows. Whatever the result I want you to be there for her, in case seeing me freaks her out.

By the way, Mr B or Black Unicorn, or whatever his ridiculous code name is, told me not to write to you, even though you are only a few wards away. But yesterday he gave me the all clear. Said you were in an isolated room anyway. He also told me that the threat from rival drug lords has started to vanish.

The word on the street is that Pretty Boy's gang has fallen apart. No way Javier is going to take his father's reins, and good for him. Javier finally showed some guts. With Pretty Boy dead he can make a better life. I hear

196

Black Unicorn has arranged for him to work at The Pastor's. Let's face it, who else would take him? He's gone in heavily disguised but apparently is doing really well there.

As for El Sapo, my lovely Papi, I've drained all his bank accounts and alerted the Mexican army of his whereabouts. I told his loyal thugs that their boss ordered Mariposa to be killed and they've now split and run. Narcos have a strict code of honor when it comes to family. Trying to kill your own child is beyond the pale even for them. And yes, I know, I've betrayed my father, something Mariposa would never do, but integrity was never my thing. So El Sapo should be banged up by the time you read this.

I've divided The Toad's money as sensibly as I can. Paid off his thugs, given a lump sum to Santiago so he can go home a wealthy man, another sum to the family of Luis Ramirez, the cop we kidnapped because he arrested Papi. Ramirez may be corrupt but his wife and kids aren't. I've bought Crazy Hawk a new Skyhawk and made donations to George and Pancho's crazy fundraising walk.

The rest will be for Mariposa. For all my faults, I'm a kick-ass bodyguard, and will dedicate myself to protecting her and her money with my life.

So, that's it. I'll be in touch soon about seeing Mariposa. Before I sign off I have to say, you looked like the biggest wimp in history when I first saw you. But you're tougher than I gave you credit for, quite the survivor. The Full Enchilada as we say out here. Oh, and please forgive me for trying to kill you several times. For what it's worth, I forgive you for bashing my brains with a crucifix.

Anyway, stop lolling about in bed, Ginger Boy, it's not as if you got shot or anything. If you can handle it, and God knows I won't blame you if you can't, I send you a hug.

Sol

Frontier of Beasts

Hal met Mariposa a week later.

He was amused that Mr B organized the event like James Bond, coordinating teams of armed, binocular-wearing DEA agents to keep an eye on things. Despite the collapse of *El Sapo*'s and Pretty Boy's empires, The Black Unicorn was still determined to take no chances.

It was an unusual get together, with Hal on the American side of the border and Rosalita, who had been staying undercover in a safe house in Tijuana, on the Mexican side. The rendezvous point was Friendship Park, an area of beach dividing the two cities of Tijuana and San Diego by means of a long, tall, steel fence.

The fence not only divided the sand between the USA and Mexico but the water too. The steel wall stretched several hundred feet out into the Pacific Ocean, and then it stopped, as if the builders erecting it had all of a sudden got out of their depth and given up.

"Built to prevent Mexicans swimming into America," explained Mr B, gesturing to the strange barrier protruding from the water. "Doesn't really work though. Fairly easy for a good swimmer to get round it." He smiled. "Or just take a boat, or maybe a tunnel under it."

Mr B pointed at the other part of the fence stretching away from the sea and over Tijuana's hills. "This border is the busiest in the world, Halford. Stretches for over 2,000 miles ending up in the Gulf of Mexico." He shook his head in awe. "Over a million people cross every day, old son, some legally, some not."

The beach was much more crowded on the Mexican side than the American. It was early evening, the Sunday before The Day of the Dead festival and a party atmosphere was brewing. Mariachis in big hats were playing trumpets. Fake grinning skulls with hats, like the ones in Pretty Boy's garage, were hanging all over the place.

The crowds on the beach swam, slept on the sand, ate tacos, slurped ice creams and flew kites. Many of them also lined up against the steel fence to meet their family or friends who lived on the opposite side of the border. They used any gaps in the barrier to chat and laugh, to hold hands, hug and kiss, do their best to ignore the steel bars dividing them.

Mr B walked with Hal to the agreed meeting point near to where the fence hit the sea. He scanned the area quickly with some miniature binoculars. As soon as Mr B saw Rosi approaching he stepped back to give the two teens some privacy. They had exchanged a few written notes but this was their first face-to-face meeting since the showdown in the desert.

Hal and Rosi rushed towards each other from opposite sides of the fence and gave themselves an awkward kiss on the cheek through the steel bars. Rosie had her hands cupped together as if holding something precious.

"Look," she whispered, opening up her fingers gently. "It's a butterfly. A monarch!" Hal admired the little creature's orange wings. "I saw it sitting on the fence." She smiled. "Some of these little beauties fly thousands of miles, all the way from Canada. They brave typhoons, rain, insect-eating birds, traffic, pollution, all just to get to Mexico."

For some reason Hal thought of Santiago and the grueling journey he had made in the opposite direction - along with thousands of others like him. He smiled, knowing at least his friend was going to be ok, Sol's money providing him and his family the chance of a better life.

"The monarchs feed on a rare type of milkweed," Rosi continued, her voice soft. "It grows in the Mexican state of Michoacán." She looked up at Hal and smiled. "My dad called me 'Mariposa' after the monarch butterfly, you know. He saw a swarm of them once when he was a kid and was blown away by how gorgeous they were. Talked about their whispering wings, like angels flying."

"Wow," said Hal, "perhaps your dad had a decent side after all."

"He used to call the border here the Frontier of Beasts," said Rosi, lost in thought. "When I was a kid I used to think it was a wonderful name. Thought it was because of all the beautiful birds, the desert foxes, the rare lizards and butterflies. I used to love reading books about them." She looked down. "Later I realized he didn't mean the animals at all." She shook her head. "He meant the human beasts –the drug lords, the gangsters, the corrupt cops." Rosi's eyes welled up. "When I understood this, it kind of broke my heart."

Rosi held up the butterfly, still cupped in her hands and threw it up. It fluttered off, gently buffeted by the breeze.

"He was right to call you after the butterfly, Rosi," said Hal, reaching for her hands through the barrier and trying to lighten the mood. "You are a beautiful beast. It suits you. For all the bad stuff, there's a lot of beauty along the border."

"No, no, I'm no beauty, no butterfly," said Rosi, her voice altered, all tense and hard. "I'm a different type of beast. The drug lord's daughter with a messed up life and a messed up face…"

"No you are *not*," Hal was surprised that he was shouting. "Don't you ever say that again in front of me, Rosi! I never, ever want to hear it!" He smashed his fists against the fence. "You are so much more than that!"

"Oh yeah, *cabroncito*," she shouted back. "Who is going to kiss this face, hey?" She pointed a finger at her cheek. "A face only a mother would kiss, that's for sure." She shot a look at Hal. "Yes, my mom, that's about it. Who else hey?"

Hal put his fingers angrily through the railings and pulled Rosi towards him. He kissed her clumsily on the nose.

"What the hell was that, *cabroncito*! Stop that right now!" Rosi pulled back from him. "What are you doing, you ginger freak?"

"I'm kissing you, Rosi." Hal continued to hold her face close and kissed her nose again, even more clumsily.

"Get off me, you crazy maniac!" Rosi aimed a wild slap at him. "Leave me alone, *cabroncito*, I'm warning you…"

"No, I won't!" said Hal, holding his ground. "I'm going to kiss you."

Rosi looked furious and utterly confused all once but she didn't pull away.

"So you want to kiss me, what a joke," said Rosi, still resisting, struggling to hold back tears. "This is ridiculous. I'm three years older than you, *cabroncito*. You have no idea what you are doing. We've got a sodding great border fence in the way…hundreds of people watching, some with binoculars…my face is a…".

"Because just maybe, Rosalita," Hal interrupted, his voice gentle but firm, "when I kiss you I don't see wounds. I see someone who is…" He kissed her nose again, gentler this time. "Brave."

He kissed her again: "Funny."

And again: "Clever."

Again: "And beautiful too, Rosi and not forgetting… crazy… stubborn… violent…"

At this point Rosi pulled Hal's face close to her. She kissed him back, gently at first, then pecking all over his face. Hal responded, pushing his face against the steel barrier to reach her.

And there the two of them stayed, looking at each other, unaware of the hundreds of other people in the background, lost in the moment. The past and the future stripped away for them, just a fierce and intimate present. It was a long time before they stepped back from each other, smiling like fools, unable to say a word.

"Thank you, *cabroncito*," Rosi whispered, finally. She sighed, nuzzling her nose back into Hal's cheek. "You crazy *chico*." They both laughed and touched their foreheads together.

"*Snow from the Moon, Dad*," thought Hal, smiling. "*Snow from the Moon*".

Mr B appeared, the red sun dipping below the Pacific behind him.

"Are you both ok?" he called out, his voice anxious. "I thought I heard some shouting." He gestured to the sky. "Besides, it's getting a bit late now."

"Talking of rare beasts, Rosi," whispered Hal, "here's the legendary Black Unicorn of Craddly Hill."

Rosalita smiled.

"I wanted to talk about so much today, *cabroncito*," she said, squeezing Hal's hand, "about Sol and Marco, Santiago and George, my Dad…and I will, but can we just leave it for now." She sighed. "It's been so hard, the last few weeks. Just for a little while let's just be kids, normal kids, I don't want to spoil this…"

Hal stepped back and looked hard into Rosi's eyes.

"Rosi, I'm sorry," he said, his voice serious. "But there is still something we really have to talk about." Hal looked behind him. "There's someone else here to see you tonight, but on my side of the fence. I'm sure it's someone who will make you happy but Mr B wasn't taking any risks." Hal turned to Mr B and nodded. "Please don't be angry with me, Rosi."

At that moment Mr B gestured behind him, ushering someone forward. In the dusky light Sol's unmistakable silhouette appeared. Hal gripped Rosi's hand and watched her face with concern.

He need not have worried. Rosalita's eyes lit up with surprise and then pure delight. "Sol!" she yelled, pushing her hands through the steel barrier as if it would magically fall apart. "Sol! Sol! Is that really you? Sol! Oh my God. Soooool!"

"I'm here Mariposa," shouted Sol, rushing towards the fence, relief on her face. "I'm here little sister!" Hal peeled away as the two sisters met in a joyous embrace. After years of fear and distrust between them, this reunion looked ecstatic: a moment of grace.

"This could take some time, old son," said Mr B, putting his arm over Hal's shoulder. "Trust me, the sun will have risen again by the time those two have finished. They've got a lifetime to catch up on."

"Now we just need to find their mum," said Hal.

"Oh, I'm ahead of the game there, Halford," replied the older man. "I tracked her down some time ago." He smiled. "I have to confess I thought Señora Ceto would either be some sort of stuck up prima donna or else a basket case."

"So, what's she like?" asked Hal.

"Carmen is one of the most lovely and intelligent women I've ever met," said Mr B, a far away look in his eye. "Completely wasted on that brute of a husband of hers."

"Way to go, Mr B," said Hal. "You really are 007 aren't you?"

"Less of your cheek, Halford," grinned Mr B. "Is that clear?"

"Crystal, Black Unicorn," replied Hal. "I'm just happy you were able to locate Rosi's mum. She'll be over the moon."

"Rosi is actually already living with Carmen in the safe house in Tijuana." Mr B explained as he walked along the beach beside Hal. "We haven't told Sol yet. Carmen still has big fears about her eldest daughter. She wanted to see how Rosi would react on knowing Sol is alive." He pointed at the border. "I chose the fence as a good location in case Rosi couldn't handle seeing her sister..."

"Well, we needn't have worried," replied Hal, watching the two sisters hugging each other through the steel border. "I think Rosi can pretty much handle anything now."

"Even you, young Halford," said Mr B, tapping his binoculars. "Don't think I didn't notice the pair of you. Purely security reasons, you understand. " He winked. "Good for you, old son."

Home

Six weeks later

Hal put on his coat, clipped Pancho's leash in place, and jogged down to Craddly Hill park. It was late autumn and the grass was coated in clumps of damp, rust-colored leaves. As soon as Hal released Pancho, the excited dog sniffed at the ground as if it was fine perfume and rolled around crazily.

Walking along the path by Craddly Hill's pond, Hal pulled a letter from his pocket. He'd only just received it and had walked to the park to read it in private. He glanced again at the handwriting, smiled, and ripped it open, hungrily scanning the words:

Cabroncito!

How's life in the wild streets of Craddly Hill? Are rival drug lords fighting for control over your Extra Strong Mints and your Dad's cod liver oil tablets?

Lots to catch up on over here, I can tell you. It's been over a month now and The Black Unicorn has finally given me the all clear to write to you.

The best news is about Mom. Mr B's organized for her to live in a remote ranch in the Sierra Madre mountains. Sol and I visit regularly. We are both so happy for her - she's like a new person, so confident. It's like we've got her back after all these years.

Mr B's also sorted out Sol with a new identity. She's now got blonde hair, funky glasses and a fake beauty spot. She looks like a tomboy, Latina version of Taylor Swift! Other than that, she's still the same old Sol, except instead of protecting Dad she's now protecting me, giving killer stares to anyone who so much as sneezes my way. We have a lot of laughs together now. And deep down –deeper than those Sierra Madre canyons! –she's got a good heart. For the first time ever I feel like I have a sister.

I should tell you about Marco. Yesterday we scattered his ashes. Sol and I were joined by Crazy Hawk, Blanca and Gabriel. We chose the waterfall where we all swam that time in the Sierra Madre. All of us cried and laughed and sang and toasted him with that disgusting corn beer Crazy Hawk likes so much. Sol and I put up a little wooden memorial to him. It reads:

SWEET DREAMS
SEÑOR MARCO 'THE NARCO' RODRIGUEZ
MUCH LOVED AND NEVER FORGOTTEN
YOUR GIRLS
SOL AND ROSI
XX

We thought "The Narco" part would appeal to Marco's sense of humor. Poor Crazy Hawk is really heartbroken about his death, but Sol and I are looking out for him. So are all his Tarahumara friends. He is really happy about his new Skyhawk though.

Did you hear about George? He's almost made it to Tijuana with Pancho on his marathon walk. That hummingbird addicted loony! The fact he's got Pancho with him has really boosted interest. Every one loves a street dog! Between them they are really going to spark interest in Miracles in Hell. The Pastor will be over the moon. Santiago also wrote. He's been able to buy a couple of trucks to start his own business. Happy days! I really miss both those guys.

But most of all, cabroncito, I miss you. I don't know why because you are definitely the worst kisser this side of the Chihuahua Desert. I mean come on, Lover Boy, you really pick your moments, don't you? My first kiss, your first kiss (I hope!) and you choose to ravish me from a different country with a 2000 mile steel barrier between us! Plus we were watched by lots of gawking sunbathers, kite flyers and Drug Enforcement Agency dudes with binoculars. What were you thinking, Romeo?!

I'm going to be honest with you, cabroncito: I've had another kiss since yours. It was Gabriel, the Tarahumara boy we met while in the Sierra Madre. Don't feel bad, my kiss with you was always going to be a one off with the age gap between us. Gabriel's about my age and he really likes me.

He's so tough but he makes me feel like I'm the most beautiful girl in the world. I can't believe my luck. And I'm sorry, but he beats you hands down when it comes to romance!

Oh, just ignore me, cabroncito, I'm only joking. It was nice kissing you too but I don't want you getting big headed! To be fair, I was trying to bash your face for the first half of it! For what it's worth, your kiss, for all its clumsiness, unlocked something in me, something I didn't think I'd ever find again. I'll always be grateful to you for that.

After my shooting by Pretty Boy, I was so angry at the world, cabroncito. I hated just about everybody who wasn't in The Miracles in Hell family. Then you come along with your punky hair and your goofy smile. I hated you at first too, trust me, despised your skinny butt! But when we were kidnapped and thrown together you grew on me. I realized I could trust you, and I hadn't trusted anyone except Marco for a long, long time.

So, what I want to say Halford George Fitzroy Bradby (what sort of snooty, melon-up-the-bum name is that by the way –I saw it on your passport!) is that I'm always on your side.

Marco said to me once that nothing in this life matters as long as you've got someone on your side. I think he was right. And well, I want you to know, my friend, no matter what life throws at you, whatever deserts you cross, oceans you swim or storms you ride, I am always on your side. Oh yes, Cabroncito, whether you like it or not, I, Mariposa Grace Ceto, have ALWAYS got your back.

I'll never forget you, you ginger freak...

Rosi

*

Hal looked up from the letter, his mind lost somewhere in the Chihuahua desert. He closed his eyes, took a deep breath, opened them again and put the letter carefully back in his coat pocket.

"Time to go home, Pancho," called Hal, looking around. "Pancho!"

Not a sign.

"Oh no," whispered Hal, starting to run. "No, no, no! No! Panchooooo."

209

He sprinted to the far side of the pond, calling his dog's name every few seconds, then started to run up Craddly Hill. Half way up he scanned the horizon and the fringing woods.

"Panchooooooo!"

"You really are the worst dog walker in the world!" said a voice behind him.

Hal span round. Gina stood under a chestnut tree holding on to Pancho's lead as he rolled in another clump of fallen leaves.

"Oh thank God!" said Hal, his whole body decompressing with relief.

Hal had not seen Gina since Mexico as, on his return home, he'd been allowed a month off school. He'd tried to call her, text, Facebook - but nothing.

"I'm glad I bumped into you," said Gina, handing Pancho's leash back. "I haven't been ignoring you. It's just that whole Mexico thing was too much to take." She gave Hal a tense look. "It's taken me a while to get my head straight."

"Oh, sure," said Hal, nodding. "No worries at all. I get it."

"I'm so happy you are ok, Hal, I really am." Gina smiled. "You can tell me what happened to you some other time. When we are both ready." She flashed her dark eyes. "You must be so pleased to be home?"

"Oh yes," said Hal. "And you too?"

"Yes, more than anything," Gina replied, her voice thoughtful. "That kidnap really shook me up. I don't want to leave Craddly Hill for a long, long time."

"I like being back," said Hal, stroking Pancho's head. "But I'm feeling kind of restless too. It's hard to explain but I think the Mexico trip really changed me – I'd love to join Dad again..." He paused. "Gina, I don't want to be rude but why didn't you get in touch? Just one quick phone call, a Get Well card..."

"I'm sorry, Hal." Gina gave him a concerned look. "It's just that JJ Masters and me are back together. I wanted to break it to you softly."

"What are you doing back with Biceps for Brains?" said Hal, shocked. "I thought he'd cheated on you with Jackie Styles?"

"JJ said it was all a huge mistake, begged to have me back," replied Gina, shrugging. "I couldn't say no. He's much more loyal than you'd think." Gina shot Hal a shy glance. "He really gave me his support after Mexico. I'm sorry, Hal, but you weren't here and he was..."

"Whatever blows the wind up your Jeans," chipped in Hal, shaking his head. "That's what they'd say on the Mexican border."

"I know you don't have much time for JJ," said Gina, "but don't be angry. No hard feelings hey?"

They both fell silent.

"No, we're cool," said Hal, finally. He gave her a swift hug. "Good luck, Gina. I'll see you back at school. Oh, and thanks for rescuing Pancho."

"Anytime and hey, for what it's worth..." she gave Hal a thumbs up, "I'm really proud of you." Gina punched Hal gently on the shoulder, turned and jogged off up Craddly Hill.

Hal watched her until she vanished out of sight. Up ahead, Pancho barked as a couple of ducks splashed into the pond.

Hal reached in his pocket for Rosi's letter. He read it one more time, smiled, then set off towards home, picking up his pace as Pancho zigzagged beside him, hot on the trail of a new scent.

"Come on, Panchito!" said Hal. "Just you and me again, boy."

Epilogue

A few months later

Chihuahua High Security Unit, Chihuahua Desert, northern Mexico

Tomas Ceto collapsed in his cell one summer's evening. Sunlight lanced across his face, lighting up his chubby cheeks and grey moustache. For a man who had lived a life steeped in blood, he looked surprisingly angelic in death.

Unlike The Toad's previous stays in prison, when he'd been able to bribe guards to provide any luxury he wanted, this latest stint behind bars had been hell – the old gangster's hopes crushed after a series of grim humiliations.

It all started one morning when he discovered outside his cell a sign with 'WORLD'S WORST FATHER' scrawled in huge, red letters, *"EL PEOR PAPÁ DEL MUNDO"*. Under it was a sketch of a butterfly and a sun. Tomas Ceto later heard Sol had paid off one the prison guards to carry out the fatal paintwork.

After this, the lonely drug lord became a target for his cellmates. His food was spat on, his head shaved and insults were shouted throughout the night. The prison guards were forced to put him in solitary confinement.

Even in seclusion The Toad knew it was just a question of time. All his family had deserted him, as had his gang of thugs. He hadn't a friend left in the world, other than Father Francisco, the prison priest.

It was this very priest, a tall, gentle, moon-faced man dressed in dark robes who now leaned over Tomas Ceto's corpse.

"He told me it was his daughter's birthday today," said Father Francisco to a stubble-cheeked prison guard waiting outside. "Poor man. The doctor diagnosed a heart attack, but he's wrong, Carlos…" The priest looked hard into Tomas's Ceto's wide eyes. "Looks like a broken heart to me"

"You gotta to be joking, father," said the guard, shaking his head. "That's The Toad. Ice for veins that one. No heart inside him."

Father Francisco looked down at Tomas Ceto's body. Stooping, he prized the drug lord's stiffened fingers apart.

Something fell to the floor.

A photo.

The priest held it up to the sunlight. The image was faded and creased from repeated viewings but the image was still clear: a young girl with marigolds in her hair at a birthday party in Mexico City. She was beaming up at her father who was looking adoringly back at her.

MY LITTLE BUTTERFLY, read the caption, *MI MARIPOSITA*.

Father Francisco smiled but his eyes were sad. He handed the photo to the guard.

"Everyone has a heart, Carlos."

THE END